T0116822

WELCOME TO
THE CLUB

Phillip Hand

iUniverse, Inc.
Bloomington

Welcome to The Club

iUniverse books may be ordered through booksellers or by contacting:

iUniverse
1663 Liberty Drive
Bloomington, IN 47403
www.iuniverse.com
1-800-Authors (1-800-288-4677)

ISBN: 978-1-4502-7827-0 (pbk)
ISBN: 978-1-4502-7828-7 (ebk)

Printed in the United States of America

iUniverse rev. date: 12/20/2010

"WHO'S THE GODDAMNED FOOL that didn't put the seat up? If I catch the piss ant, he won't have anything to pee with." It was Peg Cavanaugh again. She shouldered her way back to the bar with the men's room door slamming loud behind her.

"What's the matter, Peg, you get your ass wet?" snickered the high-pitched whiny voice of Sammy Griney. Peg picked up the kewpie-doll little man and glared into his toothless grin. "You turd!" she bellowed and sent him skidding across the floor until he came to an abrupt halt against the wall under the pinball machine.

Welcome to The Club.

That wasn't really its name. That was just the tag put on it by a couple of the young guys who stopped there about every night for a couple of beers before going on to bigger and better things in Binghamton or Scranton. They called it that because it was just the opposite of those expensive, snooty places with stuffed leather chairs and old gents walking around with trays.

And the membership was just about as opposite as you could get from the bankers, utility presidents, doctors, lawyers and car dealers who belong to those kinds of places because they think rubbing money against money begets money.

The Club was certainly exclusive. No doubt about that. It was exclusive to a certain caliber of person who would dare to be caught dead in the place. It was exclusive to those who had long since given up trying to kid anybody and who were trying to cope with life on terms they would change if they could, but knew they couldn't and knew it was all they were going to get.

It was the mid-1950s and The Club was right in the middle of the small borough of Mill Town in northeastern Pennsylvania. There were only two streets that ran the mile-long length of it and The Club was on the main one. It was next to the town library and provided an incongruity one night a month as the respectable ladies on the library board hurried into their house of books trying to ignore the beer-tipped sawmill hands tromping their way into The Club.

It was a nondescript building, two stories high but narrow with drab gray and burgundy asphalt shingles. Three concrete steps got you in the front door. A long bar was to the right as you came in and a series of red booths hugged the wall to the left. A handful of tables were scattered about and a few feet past the bar was the door to the kitchen. To the right of that was an open area that contained a small pool table. Just beyond that was the door to the bathroom. It was supposed to be the men's room, but the only place for the ladies to pee was in the vacant apartment upstairs so they all said to hell with it and used the men's room.

Walking into The Club was an adventure. You never knew what you were going to find, but you could always be sure that you wouldn't find it anywhere else. It held a collection of doers and don'ters, hopers and hopeless and some who wouldn't be there if they felt comfortable anywhere else. But they were what they were and nothing was going to change that.

The proprietor-peace keeper-ball buster-money lender-father confessor-resident philosopher of the place was Johnny Sovich. He was a professor of the people, having spent most of his life observing them, enjoying them and wondering why they do the things they do. He sometimes thought he had the answers and liked to ruminate on it but other times would just shake his head in bewilderment. Whatever they were, he enjoyed them and they thought he was about the greatest guy in the world. He had spent most of his 50-odd years a bachelor working as a master carpenter and cabinet maker. His craft had allowed him to travel a lot and his bachelorhood had allowed him the freedom to get into places and situations not privy to a married or righteous man. Johnny had been around.

He had spent most of his casual time pouring money over a bar from the wrong side. Being a generous person, he was always buying drinks for anyone who could carry on a conversation and he always kept his eye out for the empty glass. He had a face that welcomed the world, a face that invited you in.

He was a good-sized man who had always kept himself in reasonable shape considering the river of beer that had gone through his system. His head was almost bald and shiny and complemented his warm mischievous eyes. His square jaw served to broaden his grin. Johnny had always wanted to own a bar of his own where he could philosophize to his heart's content and when the little place on Main Street came on the market he grabbed it. He fixed it up nice but not so nice that he would scare off the wonderful collection of characters who didn't feel at ease in the nicer places in town.

Johnny had a lot of things going for him, but the best thing about him is that he took you on your own terms. If you were a drunk, he didn't preach to you about something you are going to do anyway. He knew that sometimes drunk is the best way to be. For some of Johnny's clients a good drunk was the only thing they had to look forward to. It kept them stacking feed, stocking shelves, cindering roads, sawing lumber, digging holes, draining cesspools, burning brush and baling hay. It took some of the sting out of the sweat in their eyes, the smart out of the broken blisters and the dull ache of boredom out of the backs of their minds. Stop at The Club and give Johnny your prescription. Better than Tylenol. For a while.

"The way I see it, the guy that's got it made is the guy that can figure out a way to stay just half drunk all the time," said Johnny, leaning on the bar and chewing a Slim Jim. "You get just the right buzz so you're still thinking good and working right, but all the shit going on doesn't bother you. The boss gives you shit, you don't care. You just 'yes, boss' him and keep on working. Your wife jumps all over your ass about fixing something, it's no problem, you just pat her fanny and talk nice and go do it. Nothing bothers you. Just the right amount of booze makes you tolerant of just about anything. Gives you all kinds of patience. You don't care if your old lady is late picking you up, you don't care if the grocery bag breaks, it don't matter if the neighbor's dog leaves a turd on your yard. You don't care. You feel good. And you know you're going to feel even better. And that's where it all goes bad.

Nobody knows how to drink just enough to keep the sun out all the time. You know what I mean? That feeling that everybody you meet is your best friend. You know they're not, but it doesn't matter, right then they're your best friend. Nobody can leave it at that. I know I can't. You always figure a few more and you'll really be on top of it. And then it all goes down the shitter. People you've been nice to get to be a pain in the ass. They disagree with you when you are right. They back into you when you are just standing there. The next thing you know, you're waking up feeling like the whole world threw up on you. If a guy could just figure out how to stay in that mellow zone, God, wouldn't it be nice?

THE WINNER AND STILL CHAMP

"You a singer? Are you a good singer? They tell me you're a singer." Henry Wabash was staring Hung Houlihan defiantly in the eye. At least he was trying to. The beer by this time had put a thin serene smile on his face and a vacant look in his eye. He could only focus for a moment and then his head would drift off to the side before swooping back to stare at Hung again. He would set his mouth in a brief challenge and then the alcohol would take over and that serene smile would come back.

"Yeah, I'm a good singer, Henry. What do you want to sing?"

"I don't care, anything," Henry said abruptly, jolting himself into full consciousness for a moment. The truth was Henry didn't sing. He hummed. And it was a regular thing with Henry to challenge anyone to sing lower than him.

"Now Henry, you can't sing lower than Hung here. He's got a natural bass voice," said Johnny, eyes twinkling as he saw some fun to be had.

"I don't give a damn what he's got. I says I can sing lower than him," said Henry, a little more alert now.

"You willing to bet a beer on it?" asked Johnny. "Damned right."

Johnny hushed the voices at the bar the way a conductor quiets down an orchestra just before the performance. He made a big thing of both of them taking a swig of beer to clear their throats and began explaining the importance of breathing properly.

"To hell with that, I know how to breathe," said Henry impatiently, but he did take the swig of beer. He had learned in his 52 years that it was important to keep his vocal cords lubricated.

"OK, Hung, You go first," said Johnny. "The rules are that you start up high and hum your way down as far as you can go. When I can't hear you anymore, you're done. Go ahead."

4

By now, everyone in the bar was gathered around listening. Hung, who got his nickname slapped on him the first time his high school teammates saw him in the shower, began humming, starting high and working his way down a note at a time. As he approached the lower registers he glanced over and saw a look of concern on Henry's face. He was very much awake now and Hung could see he was silently humming along with him. Hung finally reached his limit with a low rumble and Johnny called time.

"You've got your work cut out for you, Henry," Johnny said. "That was low."

Henry just smiled. He had drifted back into his Budweiser reverie, content that he had it locked up. "Your turn, Henry," Johnny said.

Henry sat straight up on the barstool and began. It was a melodious hum with a full resonating tone and he slid it down note by note with definition. Each time he lowered the note he also lowered his head. It wasn't long before his chin was level with the bar and Johnny also had to put his chin on the bar to be able to hear the notes. A couple of more notes and you couldn't see Henry's eyes anymore. Johnny was looking at his forehead. And then only the top of Henry's sandy-haired head could be seen as he reached even further into the bass register. But he was still humming. Johnny sprawled across the bar and dipped his head down the other side in an effort to measure Henry's dirge. Finally there was silence. Johnny pulled himself upright and said, "Sorry, Hung, but Henry's still the champ. Way to go Henry – Henry?"

Henry's head never did come back up. He was all bent over as if he was trying to tie his shoe on the barstool. His head was braced against the side of the bar and then it began a slow slide toward the floor. The rest of Henry followed along and hit the floor with a soft thump.

"Well, look 'a there," said Johnny. "Henry's hummed himself to sleep."

SOME THINGS ARE JUST PLAIN SACRED

"Hey, Johnny,-click-,how about-click-setting a-click-quart of-click-beer-click-up here-click-so I-click-can prime-click-the-pump?" They don't come much bigger than Dana Harford. He wasn't so much tall as he was just big. Everything about him was big. Even his ears looked powerful. His huge head fastened to a bull neck and the rest of him just kept growing out. Huge chest and even bigger belly. He was thick all over. His arms were as big as fire logs, and he couldn't get both hands into a gunny sack at the same time. He was a farmer and seemed to live in his coveralls. He stopped in at The Club every time he came into town to buy feed and his wife dreaded the trips. She was a mousey little woman who was a born-again whatever and hated drink. She could keep a pretty good rein on Dana out on the place, but he left her and everything about her when he came to town.

Dana was an easy-going guy and well-liked, but the one thing about him that drove everybody nuts was the clicking of his teeth. He had a full set of ill-fitting choppers that just didn't want to sit still. Every time he talked they jumped right off his gums and when he laughed it was like shaking a box of chicklets.

"Another-click-quart there,-click-Johnny,I'm-click-dyin'-click-over-click-here," Dana bellowed. Johnny set up two quarts just to make sure Dana didn't drop dead on the spot.

"How you been, Dana?" It was Willard Klemp, a fast-talking potato chip deliveryman who stopped in daily to deliver his newest dirty joke. The problem was he told the joke to every new person who came in so if you were the first guy in that day, you probably heard the joke about 20 times until it wasn't funny anymore. But Willard laughed as hard the 20th time as he did the first.

"I've-click-been-click-fine," Dana said.

"My God, why don't you do something with those teeth," Willard said, as Dana was draining the last few drops of his fourth quart of beer. "You ought to glue them down or something."

"They're-click-OK. I-click-don't-click-have-no-click-trouble-click-with-click-them," said Dana, as the beer began to slow down his ponderous brain. He swilled down another quart.

After awhile Willard saw Dana was getting settled heavy on the barstool and decided to risk some fun. He winked over at Glenn Tink and Shake Ketter and turned to Dana. "Let me see them things. Maybe I can stretch 'em a little, make 'em fit better."

"Well-click-OK-click, but-click-be careful. They're-click- the-click-only things-click-I got-click-to-click-eat with." He took out the teeth and handed them to Willard. His cheeks and lips caved in as though they were being sucked back into his mouth. "Nu, fon't wop fem," he said, his tongue and lips getting all tangled up together and strangling his word. "Hell, all they need is a good bath," said Willard and he dipped them in a pitcher of beer. "Hey, fon't fo hat," said Dana, "Hive hem hack." But by now Willard had passed them along the bar to Glenn. "Look at those beauties, Glenn, not a cavity in 'em."

Glenn was afraid of Dana but he was more afraid that the others would think he was afraid so he went along with it. "They're nice choppers, all right," holding them up in front of him with two fingers. "There's a lot of chewin' left in them," and he passed them on to Shake just as Dana reached for them.

"Hod damn hou. Hiv hem hack wight dow," Dana said, but Glenn had already slipped them to Shake.

Shake inspected the teeth carefully, turning them over in his hands, and then proceeded to walk along the bar showing them to everyone in the place. Dana made a couple of moves to get up and go after them, but by now the several quarts of beer he had drained convinced him that it just wasn't worth the effort. He was comfortable where he was and he felt like he could sit there all day. But he did want his teeth back.

"Fring hem heeth hown here wight how, Sake," he threatened, his lips flapping against his gums. But Shake could also see that Dana was rooted to the barstool and he wasn't about to end the fun right away. He held the teeth at arms length. "I always wondered how these things worked," he said and crammed them into his mouth. He stood there with a grotesque double grin on his already ugly face looking like something out of a horror movie. Shake was odd enough looking with just his own teeth, but with Dana's set forcing his mouth open and stretching his cheeks, he was ready for Halloween. With some effort, he managed to get his lips closed over the teeth. Most of those along the bar were either grimacing in disgust or were roaring at Shake's appearance. But Peg Cavanaugh had been on the phone and as she walked back to the bar, Shake motioned for the others not to say anything.

Peg slid her sturdy frame onto the stool and proceeded to light a cigarette. Shake walked up behind her quietly and tapped her on the shoulder. She turned and Shake suddenly flashed her a hideous grin. Peg let out a shriek and threw up her hands, dropping a full glass of beer. The place was in an uproar, everyone enjoying Peg's terror. It took about five seconds for Peg to realize what was going on and only a fraction of that for her to nail Shake with an open-handed haymaker on the left side of his jaw.

Dana's teeth flew out of Shake's mouth like two clay pigeons out of the trap at a skeet shoot. The uppers landed on the floor and skidded under a radiator. The lowers bounced off the side of Glenn's head and plopped right into the gallon jar of pickled eggs. Shake retrieved the uppers from under the radiator and brushed the dirt off them, and Johnny fished the lowers out of the jar with a pair of tongs. " These must be made of iron, not a nick in them," Shake said, somewhat relieved that they weren't broken.

The bedlam subsided to a few chuckles and they heard the sobbing. Heavy sorrowful sobs coming out of Dana's huge frame. His head was down and tears ran down his cheeks.

" Hey, Dana, it's all right. The teeth didn't break. Look," and Johnny held both sets under the beer tap to rinse them off before handing them back to the weeping giant. Everyone was unnerved by the sight of the powerful figure crying like a baby.

Dana took the teeth from Johnny and put them clumsily into his mouth. He didn't want to cry in front of all these people, but the beer wouldn't let him stop. It had a hold on him and wouldn't let go. He did manage to slow it down to some sniffles and Johnny handed him some tissues to make himself presentable.

"What the hell's the matter, Dana?" Johnny said. "It's just a pair of teeth." "No-click-it-click-ain't," Dana sobbed. "They-click-was-click-the only-click-thing-click-my Uncle Bert-click-had-click-left-click-to his-click-name-click-when he-click-got-click-run over-click-by the-click-manure spreader-click-and-click-he-click-passed 'em-click-on-click-to me."

A MAN OF PURPOSE

STARLEY BASIL CAME INTO The Club and headed straight for the kitchen. He didn't look right or left or offer a greeting. His was a purposeful stride. He had a mission. His mission was to mop the floor. He returned in moments with a mop and pail with a fancy wringer on it and brought the pail over to the bar for Johnny to fill with hot, soapy water. Starley was a pathetic looking creature. Everything he wore was too big for him. Pants, shirt, coat, shoes, everything. He looked as if someone had let all the air out of him after he had gotten dressed. The clothes just hung on him.

He had been a big man at one time, but too many bars and a couple of enduring gifts from carnival women had left him looking like a concentration camp survivor. The skin on his drawn face hung loose, folding into a chicken neck. There was nothing to be seen of him beyond that because Starley wore his dirty flannel shirt buttoned to the neck even on the hottest summer days. His coverall jacket had grown heavy with sweat and grime over the years and was stiff enough to stand by itself. Starley's eyes set deep in their sockets, sad but with a hint that there were warm memories behind them. He looked as if he should be the unhappiest man alive, but he was just the opposite. He was seldom seen without a cockeyed grin on his face. Half his teeth were gone and the others were hanging on for their dear decayed lives, but it was such a warm grin that you overlooked the rot.

"There's the smartest man in this town," said Johnny to a visitor who was just passing through, as Starley mopped back and forth with long, slow, wet strokes. " He knows his limits."

Starley dipped the mop in the pail, squeezed it and continued methodically. "He comes in here every afternoon and mops this floor in exchange for enough beer to get him through the night. You watch him. Everything has to be just so. He won't mop around the tables. He moves them. Gets right back into the corners. Anything on the floor the mop won't get, he scrapes it off with a knife. Everything gets moved, everything goes back in exactly the right place. You watch, when he gets through, he'll walk through here like a general inspecting an Army barracks. When he is satisfied, he'll take his seat down there at the corner of the bar and watch everyone else make fools of themselves."

Starley finished up and did just as Johnny said. Satisfied with his inspection, he slid onto a stool against the wall and waited. He didn't order, just waited. Johnny poured a beer and took it down to him. "Nice job, Starley," he said, "Looks good." Starley grinned proudly despite the fact Johnny told him the same thing every day.

Johnny came back and leaned on the bar. "You know why he's the smartest man in town? Because he is satisfied with what he's got. How many people do you know who are satisfied with what they've got? Nobody. Everybody wants more. More money, more recognition, more power, more vacation, more friends, more of this, more of that. We live lives of more. Everything is geared to it. They make you feel guilty if you don't want more. You're a failure if you don't want more.

"But Starley, he's got what he wants. A little food from the kitchen and enough beer to get by on and most important of all, he's got a purpose. Starley has a reason for being here. That floor, that's his purpose. And the smartest thing of all is that he's got something he knows he can do. You know what I mean? He knows he can do a damn good job on that floor and be content with that. He's not looking to try things that will just get him bent all out of shape because he can't do them.

"You ever notice that? How people get real good at something and then they take on something else and have to start all over again and get all uptight and frustrated because they're trying to do something they don't know how to do. Everybody's expected to keep trying to do more than they can do right now. What's wrong with learning how to do one thing good and leaving it at that? You do one thing, someone else does something else and so on until everything is covered. You get up every day knowing you can handle it. Not a bad feeling. The way I see it, if everybody could make up their minds that they would be satisfied with just so much, You know, put a cutoff on it, and then say, OK, that's it, I don't want any more, and if they would learn to do one thing real good and let it go at that, then we'd all be as smart as old Starley down there."

THE BATTLE OF THE TITANS

"You never saw the day you could whip me and you never will." Shake Ketter drew back from the bar and focused a liquid eye on Ed Hooker. Ed, filled with 90 proof courage, also stepped back and squared off toward Shake. It looked like a Western shootout.

"Come on, you bastard, I'll take you on," Ed challenged and he spit on both of his hands and rubbed them together.

"I'll drop you with one shot," said Shake.

"In a pig's ass, you will," said Ed.

"By God, you've had it, said Shake.

"Horseshit," said Ed.

They glared at each other still about 10 feet apart. Shake was about as mean and ugly looking as you could get. He stood there with his huge arms and stomach bulging out of his old green army T-shirt. He was well over 200 pounds and all of it looked mean. But there was nothing meaner than his face. It was big and round and red with a jagged scar running from just under his left eye down near the corner of his mouth. He had another smaller scar coming out of the corner of his right eye. Four or five of his bottom front teeth were gone and his big whisky nose leaned sharply to the left. His hands were big and meaty and his fingers looked like stuffed sausages. He was ready to do battle.

Ed was almost as big and almost as ugly. His forehead started with two big bushy eyebrows and slanted sharply toward the back of his head as though he had been cheated of a fair portion of brain matter, which was true. Where Shake's eyes were tight and squinty, Ed's eyes were open almost too wide, as though he were in a perpetual state of surprise. His thick mouth hung open most of the time, adding to the look of astonishment on his face. He was wearing his red plaid hunting jacket that he carried on his back most of his waking hours. He tried to glare at Shake, but his drooping mouth and his bug eyes made him look more perplexed than menacing. But he was ready.

The fact was that, as big and ugly as they were, neither had ever won a fight. Ed had lost more because he had been in more. He had the edge on Shake in experience, but it was all bad. He was a more experienced loser, but Shake had the distinction of never having been witnessed even being able to land a punch. His pugilistic style was to get his arms out in front of him and to make slow windmill motions with his fists. He would then circle around and around his opponent until the guy got tired or bored or both and would pop Shake on the button and down he would go. End of fight.

Ed was more cautious. He didn't circle. He would get both fists up in front of his face and just stand there. He was more of a counter puncher except he never quite got to the counter. The punching he got, the countering he never quite pulled off. The flaw in his defense was that he kept his hands smack in front of his eyes so he couldn't see anything. He couldn't see the guy he was fighting let alone the punches coming. The guy could walk around Ed and belt him in the back of the head and Ed would still be standing there with his hands blocking out everything except the other guy's fists. Just about everyone in town had whipped Ed, including little Sammy Griney who had to drag over a chair and stand up on it to finish Ed off. You could call Ed a statuesque fighter because he had about as much movement as the stone figure of William Penn in Mill Town's downtown park. At any rate, the two of them were ready to put their unblemished loss records on the line after a nonsensical argument one night in The Club. Johnny knew there was no fear of any serious damage to either combatant so he didn't try to stop it. The two of them stood there squared away at each other as the customers lined up for their barside seats. Shake and Ed stood just outside arms harm from each other and up came Shake's fists and his slow windmill motion.

Up came Ed's fists in front of his eyes. He couldn't see a thing. Shake was about to start his circling tactic when he noticed his cigarettes rolled up in the sleeve of his T-shirt.

"Wait a minute," he said," I don't want to break these." He took them out and handed them to Peg Cavanaugh. "Here, you can have one for holding them, but that's all," he said. While this was going on, Ed was still standing there with his fists in front of his face, seeing nothing.

Shake started his windmill motion again and began to circle. It was Ed's turn.

"Hold it. I'm takin' this coat off, Can't get full use of my arms in it." He struggled to get out of the heavy mackinaw and finally backed up to the bar where Petey Slater took a hold of it and peeled it off his back. Ed stepped back out in the middle of the floor, brought his fists back up in front of his eyes, made sure he couldn't see anything and proceeded to stand there. By this time the fight fans were growing restless and began shouting for some action.

Shake obliged. He began slowly circling his quarry, looking for his opening. By the time he got around behind Ed he had all the opening in the world, but he apparently decided to play it safe. He kept circling until he had to detour around the large metal post that stood in the middle of the floor holding up the ceiling. He got around the post and then continued to get around Ed. It was a slow motion stalking much like the last few steps of a lion before it pounces. But Shake never pounced. He just kept circling.

By the time Shake had gone around Ed for the fifth time, the crowd was in hysterics. The tears were running right down Johnny's face. But Ed and Shake were so absorbed in their fight strategies that they barely noticed. The tension was beginning to get to Ed and the sweat broke out on his forehead. A couple of salty beads ran down into his right eye and he reached to wipe it.

Shake thought it was Ed's big counter attack and he threw his head back to avoid the haymaker. When he did he banged the back of it full force against the metal post. A puzzled look crossed his face just before he pitched forward, crashing nose down on the floor. He didn't move a muscle.

Ed stood there in his defensive stance a few moments more before lowering his hands cautiously to see what the big noise was. He saw Shake out cold in front of him.

"That'll teach the bastard," he said and walked proudly over to receive the congratulations of the crowd. His first win.

WE'VE ALL GOTTA BE GOOD AT SOMETHING

"WHO THE HELL DID that?" Johnny asked, wrinkling his nose in disgust at the repugnant vapor hanging heavy in the bar. It was enough to melt a crow bar.

"Jesus, somebody's carryin' a dead skunk around in his ass," said Donkey Nuts Crowley, a man not known to mince words. And if Donkey Nuts thought it was bad, you knew it was bad because he was one of the all-time best air blasters in Susquehanna County.

As the odor crept along the bar like a slow-moving grass fire, one head after another came to attention with a pained grimace and a look right and left trying to spot a telltale sign that would convict the culprit. As everyone bitched and accused everyone else about the stench, Johnny glanced along the bar to his right and saw Sammy Griney trying to look nonchalant, but with a sly, satisfied smirk creasing his face. He was the only one not squawking and that's what did him in. It is the sure fire way to pinpoint a fart felon. He's reluctant to say anything, always hoping that no one will notice even if the smell is strong enough to peel the paper off the walls.

"Sammy, you little shit, was that you?" Johnny demanded. "No, hell no, it wasn't me," Sammy squeaked defensively. But it was no use. The farter can never deny it convincingly because at the end of even the most vocal and defiant protestation there comes that convicting smirk. He doesn't truly want them to think it was someone else. Pride of authorship or something like that.

After everyone had properly castigated Sammy, the conversation turned to one of serious farting. Donkey Nuts started it by declaring he could not understand how you could anatomically get such a huge smell out of such a sawed-off soul as Sammy. "Size don't mean a damn thing," said Glenn Tink.

14

"It's what you eat. I'm skinny as a rail fence, but when I get down about a head of boiled cabbage, I can blow down a barn."

"I think it's in them gene things," said Shake Ketter thoughtfully. "Some people are just better at it and I think they just inherit it. You know, like buck teeth or somethin.'"

"No, it's the beer that does it," said Willard Klemp. He held up his glass. "Look at all those bubbles comin' up. You gulp those down and what the hell you think is going to happen? They're going to come out somewhere and there's only two ways they can go."

"By God, I got mine trained. I can let 'em fly any damn time I want to," said By God Harry Hollis. His name was Harry Hollis but everyone knew him as By God Harry because he didn't even say hello without sticking a By God in front of it. "By God, I can damn near make 'em play a tune," he said proudly. There were eight or nine guys in the bar and they soon became embroiled in a serious discussion of flatulence and what goes into making a good fart. After hearing By God Harry's boasts, they also began to trumpet their own gaseous talents. It was all Johnny needed. He figured Sammy had already stunk the place up so much that he might as well make the most of it by having a little fun.

"OK, you guys, put your money where your ass is. We're going to have a contest. Everybody put up a buck and you all get your turn. Three farts apiece if you can make 'em. If you can't get three, we'll go by your best effort." There was an immediate show of interest by Donkey Nuts and a couple of others who knew they had a good chance of winning. Several others entered just to be polite and they each placed a dollar in front of them on the bar.

"How you going to judge them, Johnny?" Donkey Nuts wanted to know. " You goin' by sound, smell or what?" "Both," Johnny said, "but you have to declare which way you're going. You can go for both if you think you are up to it and, if you do, it will count more. Degree of difficulty, you know, like in the Olympics."

It was agreed that Donkey Nuts would go first. That agreement was reached because Donkey Nuts said he wanted to go first and nobody in his right mind was going to argue it. He was built like a gorilla from his face on down. His shoulders sloped. There were no square corners on him and there was also no fat. He had incredible coordination and athletic grace. He was a natural athlete and excelled at any sport he got involved in. He got his name one night when he loudly declared that he was horny enough to romance a burro if he could grab onto something that would make it hold still. At any rate, he was putting his athletic ability on the line as he stepped back from the bar. He turned his back to the bar and a sudden howl of protest went up.

"No fair, he's aiming it at us!" cried a panicky Glenn Tink. Sammy had already scrambled down off the bar stool out of the range of fire. Willard Klemp tripped over By God Harry trying to get out of the way. "Wait a minute, Donk," Johnny said. "In the interest of fair play and survival, point it the other way. Besides, I just put a new mirror up here," pointing behind the bar, " and I don't want it getting all fogged up." Once they got Donkey Nuts sighted down range, he began to apply himself. Strain lines creased his forehead, concentration forced his eyes about half closed and his entire body tensed up as though he had grabbed hold of an electric fence. All of a sudden there came a long ripping sound like someone tearing heavy canvas. It lasted at least two to three seconds. Then the aroma, enough to make your eyes smart. A major league fart. "God, did that one burn. Must have been those hot peppers, " Donkey Nuts said and slid tenderly back onto his bar stool.

The others tried to shake their heads clear of Donkey Nuts' gassing and got ready for the next contestant. It was to be Glenn Tink. As Glenn had said earlier, he was skinny. There was just about enough of him to say he was there and that was all. He was in his mid-30s, had a lean, not bad-looking face and a passion for white-haired women over 70. His track record wasn't too good, but he never passed up a chance at any female with a Social Security check and a bottle of Geritol in her purse. He claimed they were more grateful at that age.

As soon as Johnny had outlined the rules of the contest, Glenn had started wolfing down pickled eggs from the gallon jar on the bar. It was sort of like loading up a cannon. He must have put down half a dozen eggs by the time Donkey Nuts took the field of battle. Glenn hurriedly slugged down as much beer as he could handle to get the eggs as far down into his stomach as possible. He stood up and walked a few feet away from the bar. He made a big thing of positioning himself just so. He checked behind him to make sure no one was in the line of fire, did a couple of deep knee bends to get things stirred up real good, and bent over and touched his toes a couple of times just to make sure there weren't any obstructions. He was hamming it up.

"By God, Glenn, fart or get off the pot," said By God Harry impatiently. He could feel his first attempt building up and he didn't want to waste it where it wouldn't be appreciated. Glenn put everything he had into it, which wasn't much. A good fart would about outweigh him. He clenched his fists and tightened every muscle in his body. His face turned flaming red and his cheeks hardened like a trumpet player's. Except he was blowing the other way. Just about the time he was ready to pass out from exertion, there came a soft, quiet "pfttt." Barely a sound. Glenn's entire body slackened. He was drained. His moment of glory was over.

"A God-damned dud," crowed Donkey Nuts. "What did you do, Glenn, put a muffler on it?" Everyone at the bar was howling at Glenn's meager effort. "My old lady farts louder than that," said Willard Klemp. Chagrined, Glenn moved quietly back to the bar and sat down. "I needed more eggs," he said softly to himself. It was about then they got it. It was a choking, breath-grabbing blanket of stink that began to cover them, a delayed-reaction bomb that Glenn's silence had not prepared them for. It was so thick and pungent you could almost feel it. Willard Klemp even tried to brush it away. "By God, that's rank," said By God Harry. "That's thick enough to paint a barn with," said Shake. "There goes my new mirror," said Johnny. Glenn's spirits began to pick up as he found himself back in the running and also back in the good graces of his competitors. Thank God for pickled eggs.

Several others took their turns in the middle of the floor with varying degrees of success. There were bleets and blats, belches and burps, but none of Major League proportions. By God Harry had a good shot at it, but he forgot he had his coveralls on over his work pants and what would have been a mighty declaration instead was smothered and contained in the seat of his britches.

Sammy had elected to pass on his earlier turns because he had about used up his ammunition on the fart that had prompted the contest in the first place and he wanted some time to reload. But his moment of truth finally arrived and he nervously took his place in the arena. Willard Klemp started laughing. "This is the case of a little fart trying to make a big fart." The others howled, but Sammy wasn't listening. He was concentrating. He stood at attention. He strained. Nothing. He brought his arms in front of him and crouched a little. More strain. Nothing. He took a deep breath, closed his mouth tight and pushed for all he was worth. Nothing. Another breath, mouth clamped shut, his small body began to shake, his face turned purple. And then … "Ohhh, Jesus!" His legs snapped together and his right hand clamped onto his ass. "Ohhh, Jesus to Jesus," his tiny, high-pitched voice wailed. "Oh, my God!" and he wiggled off toward the men's room as fast as he could go with his hand on his ass and his legs tight together as though they were tied with bailing wire.

The Club was in an uproar. They could hear Sammy behind the door cursing rapidly as he ripped long gobs of toilet paper off the roll. "Well, what do you think? " Donkey Nuts asked Johnny as they waited for Sammy to make his repairs. Donkey Nuts was eyeing the dollar bills on the bar and adding them up silently.

"I don't know," Johnny said. "It isn't all that easy. I wish I had a meter or something. No doubt about it, you had the loudest one. But Glenn's had to be the rottenest one. And By God Harry would have been right up there if he'd thought to take his coveralls off. What about Sammy? He deserves some kind of a consolation prize."

About that time, Peg Cavanaugh walked into the bar and headed for the kitchen to make an onion sandwich for herself. She came back along the bar chomping on the sandwich and nodded hello to everyone. As she passed by them, her big frame shuddered abruptly and she dropped a bomb that sounded like a sonic boom. A 5.0 on the Richter scale. She left a vapor trail that was a real window opener. An eye-stinging, belly-turning, weed-killing, cancer -causing chemical reaction. "Sorry about that, boys," Peg said as she went down to the other end of the bar and signaled for a beer.

Donkey Nuts looked at Glenn, Glenn looked at By God Harry, they all looked at Johnny and they all got up, picked up their dollar bills and one by one filed past Peg and without a word dropped the money in front her. They left the puzzled gold medalist to enjoy her beer.

MA, WHY DIDN'T YOU TEACH ME TO DANCE?

"THOSE HAVE GOT TO be the eighth and ninth wonders of the world," said Willard Klemp. He was staring straight into Peg Cavanaugh's breasts. It was the first thing Willard did every time he came into The Club with his supply of cigarettes. Fill up the machine, order a beer and position himself so he had an unobstructed view of Peg's globes. He was mesmerized by them. He didn't steal glances the way most of the guys did. He locked in eyeball to nipple and barely blinked. He could carry on a conversation with people on both sides of him, even get into shouting matches about this or that, and never take his eyes off Peg's chest.

"Did you ever see anything like that in your life, Johnny?" Willard asked incredulously. "They are monsters."

"Well, I'm not sure monsters is exactly the right word, but they are a piece of work," Johnny replied. He was as aware of Peg's proportions as anyone, having spent countless hours pushing beers across the bar at her.

Peg was well aware of her attributes as well and just as aware of the effect on the male members of The Club. She wore T-shirts in the summer and sweaters in the winter. There was nothing petite about Peg. She was a big woman, almost to the point of being mannish. She was just under six feet tall, broad shouldered and strong.

Her face was a bit rough cut, but attractive. If her features had been softened a little, she could have been called pretty. Her body was surprisingly well proportioned for a woman her size. She was big but in the right places. She liked to wear bright colors and went heavy on the lipstick. For some reason, she always wore bright red lipstick and wore it thick. You always knew what beer glass Peg had been drinking from because it always looked as though someone had used it to slit his throat. Lots of red.

Peg, despite her curves and lipstick, was one of the boys. She could "By

19

God" with the best of them and took no nonsense from anyone. The regulars in The Club had long since learned not to get her mad and had also learned that you didn't come on to Peg. You waited and hoped that she wanted to come on to you. Peg was married to an overweight layabout who was regularly trying to sum up the strength to look for work, but it was an indifferent relationship, which is to say Peg would buy him a beer if he came into the bar but would seldom go home with him.

Peg had no reluctance to occasionally enjoy herself with someone she took a liking to, but it was always on her terms. Most of the time she spent on the corner barstool, drinking beer, playing the jukebox and trying to get Sammy Griney to dance.

And while Peg sat, everyone else stared at her jugs. They were round and so full that there was almost no separation between them. Her cleavage started at her Adam's apple. They came straight out of her chest like an advance guard. Willard could barely stand it.

"My God, those are milkers," he said, looking longingly at Peg's light, summer sweater stretched to its limits. "What I wouldn't give…"

"Forget it, Willard, " said Johnny. "She already told you she can't stand you. You know what'll happen if you push it."

"Yeah, I know. I'm not that crazy." He had accepted Peg's rejection of him with reluctance. He had made his move on her one night when he was about half greased and willing to risk whatever questionable future he had for a shot at those breasts. He almost got a handful before Peg got him by the hair on the top of his head and rammed him into the bar.

She pulled him back up, looked him in the eye and said, "Willard, you are the sorriest bull turd asshole I've ever seen." She shoved him away and he took her evaluation back to his barstool, more upset that he had come up just inches short of Nirvana than he was at his splitting headache or her pronouncement, or the jeers of the other men who wished they dared get as close as Willard did.

But now Willard kept his distance and just stared. Peg had long since resigned herself to his attention and put up with it as long as he didn't make any more foolish moves.

"I tell you, Johnny, and I'm not going to do anything, mind you, but I would dearly love to see those things out in the open. You could strike me blind after that and I would have seen it all." Willard was musing and staring when Donkey Nuts Crowley walked in. "How the hell are ya, Willard?" he asked.

"I'm fine, Donk, but I'd be a lot finer if I could bury my face in those," he said nodding toward Peg.

"Yeah, they're somethin' ain't they? Well, why don't you do somethin' about it. Sweet talk her a little bit. You've got about as good a line of shit as anybody I know."

"I guess you didn't hear what happened the last time I tried to get next to her. She damn near killed me. I'm not going to go through that again."

"Willard, you got to know how to approach 'em," Donkey Nuts instructed. "It ain't only what you say, it's how you say it. Women are all about the same that way. They all want to have men fallin' all over their ass, but they don't like to admit it. They want you to be cute and suave like you was talkin' to a real lady."

"I don't think that would work with Peg," Willard said. "She's pretty set about who she's going to mess around with."

"Bull shit, I could smooth talk her right out of her pants," Donkey Nuts said.

"I'd just like to see you talk her out of her sweater. That would be enough for me," Willard said wistfully.

Willard watched as Donkey Nuts moved close to Peg and began talking softly. Peg replied and they talked back and forth for a couple of minutes. And then Willard saw Donkey Nuts say something and saw Peg rare back and nail him with a straight right to the chops. If it had been anyone other than Donkey Nuts, he would have gone down for sure. But he managed to keep his feet. He thought of giving her a shot back but could see she was not about to back off and realized what it would look like if he hit a woman – even as big as Peg. So he rubbed his jaw and walked back down the bar to where Willard was enjoying the whole thing.

"What in hell happened?" Willard asked. "It looked like things were going real good there."

"They was," Donkey Nuts said. "She seemed real friendly right up until I asked her how she'd like to nurse a 32-year-old baby." Peg was still steaming when someone punched out "Rock Around the Clock" on the juke box and the bar filled with loud, driving music. Peg loved to dance and wasn't a bit bashful about stepping out on the floor and dancing all by herself. She did just that as Willard and Donkey Nuts watched. She was light on her feet for her size and had a real bounce to her step.

And when Peg bounced, she bounced. It looked like someone dribbling two basketballs in front of her.

"Do you see that?" Willard frothed. "Do you see that? Isn't that somethin'" Isn't that somethin' else? I don't believe it."

"You can believe it," Donkey Nuts replied. "They've got to be real or they wouldn't bounce like that. I just wish she wasn't so damn hard to get along with," he said as he rubbed his jaw.

Peg danced over to where Sammy Griney was trying to decide whether to blow his next to last dollar on Johnny's baseball pool or save it for beer later on.

"C'mon Sammy, let's dance," Peg said. It was a thing with her to get Sammy on the dance floor. She thought there was something cute about the little guy struggling around the floor with his nose at about the level of her belly button and she tried to drag him out there every chance she got. But Sammy hated it. He didn't know how to dance and he felt like a hog in an auction pen every time he got stuck out there with everyone looking at him. He always resisted furiously, but Peg sometimes wouldn't take no for an answer. This was one of those times.

"C'mon Sammy, let's do it."

"No, I don't want to dance," he squeaked.

"Aw, C'mon, I'll lead."

"No, damn it, Peg, I'm not goin' to do it. Just leave me alone."

"I want to dance, Sammy, now you c'mon."

"I said "no", By God, and when I say "no" I mean "no", and there ain't no more to say about it 'cause that's it and ..."

"You little shit, you're going to dance," bellowed Peg as she grabbed him by the armpits, lifted him off the stool and carried him onto the floor.

"You put me down, Peg!" he screeched, his feet dangling six inches above the floor as Peg whirled him around. He squirmed and twisted but Peg had a lock on him. "Cut this shit out!".

Peg kept right on dancing, ignoring his squeals. She whirled in circles and Sammy's feet flew out behind him like the swing on one of those carnival rides that keeps going faster and faster until they are straight out. She kept circling the floor and then she spotted Willard and Donkey Nuts grinning at Sammy's plight.

She slowed down and let Sammy's feet touch the floor. "You just bashful about being out here in front of everybody?" she asked. "You afraid everybody's going to see you? Well, I can fix that," and she pulled her sweater out of her slacks, stretched it forward and brought it down over Sammy's head. She then wrapped her arms around him, lifted him off the floor and began dancing again. His face was pressed deep into those two mounds of flesh. At first he started wiggling and thrashing his head back and forth because it was hard to breath. But he soon stopped struggling and began concentrating his efforts on trying to see those enormous appendages that were damn near smothering him. He tried to pull his head back and take a look, but the sweater was so tight that he could barely get his nose out of the cleavage. So close to one of the monumental sights of all time and Sammy couldn't see a thing.

But Willard could see just fine and he was going crazy. "Look at that! Just look at that!" he shouted. "Oh, my God, I don't believe it. That little son of a bitch. Look at him. How the hell does he rate?"

"I hope he knew enough to get his mouth open," said Donkey Nuts.

Peg finally decided that Sammy had had enough and that Willard had had enough and when there came a break in the music she allowed Sammy's head to escape from under her sweater. Not that Sammy was rushing to go anywhere. When she slowly peeled her sweater off the back of his neck, his hairs were standing right up on end. He just stood there hoping that maybe it would start all over again. But Peg was done. She bent down to Sammy and whispered, "You greedy little shit. I'm sure glad you don't have any teeth."

Sammy walked a little taller in The Club after that.

A GAME OF NO CHANCE

"Anybody wanna play checkies?" Petey Slater was broke again. He walked into The Club with his checkerboard under his arm and proceeded down the bar. You always knew when Petey was around, partly because of his annoying cackling voice, but mostly because of the strong smell of fresh cut wood. Petey worked in the sawmill that was only a short distance down the street from The Club and he always looked and smelled as though he had taken half of it home with him. He was short, with a slight build and the pinched face of a weasel. Most of his teeth had long since abandoned him and the few that were left had soaked up more than their share of tobacco juice. No one could ever recall seeing Petey when he was not covered with a fairly thick dusting of shavings and sawdust. He wore it in his hair the way some women wear that sparkly, glittery stardust. All of the sawmill guys carried some sign of their work on them, but most of them at least washed it off on Saturday nights. Not Petey. He hadn't seen the deep side of a bathtub in years so it was sort of a blessing that he did carry around the scent of fresh cut pine. It could have been a lot worse.

Petey was a regular at The Club and spent most of his meager wages dime by dime on draft beers. He had a family back up in the hills outside of town that he more or less took care of depending on how much he had left after his visit to The Club. He was as tightfisted as they come and when he would pay for a beer, he would reach into his pocket and thumb the coin from his hand like someone lining up a tiddley wink. You never saw any of Petey's money laying on the bar. His financial holdings were always a mystery. Always, that is, until he would come through the door with his checkerboard under his arm. Then you knew Petey Slater was broke.

If nothing else, he was a survivor. Blessed with a brain that would make a sloth look like a whiz kid, he had an uncanny ability to play checkers and win.

He couldn't even spell checkers, but when it meant the difference between winning and losing a 10-cent beer, he was invincible. He was so good that Johnny even let him compete on credit. He wouldn't let Petey run a bar tab because he had enough trouble squeezing money out of him as it was, but Johnny knew that in a checker game someone else was almost always going to pay.

So Petey could come into The Club flat broke, drink more than he could hold and stagger out not owing a dime. There was always someone to take him on. Some played him just to watch the contortions he would go through and the devious means he would use to win.

Petey was not one bit above cheating, and did so at every opportunity. He had perfected an elbow slide with which he could move a checker three spaces without being detected by anyone less than the most alert opponent. There were a myriad of distractions in The Club and Petey got away with murder. Which is not to take away from his ability to win honestly. If he had to, and he often did, he could beat just about anyone fair and square. He just found it easier and more in his nature to cheat. When his honesty was questioned, he would howl and carry on as though someone had insulted his mother. Most felt Petey was the biggest insult his mother could ever have endured, and some didn't mind letting him know it, but it never bothered him as long as he could gleefully holler, "King me!"

Petey's most effective strategy for victory was his patented slow down. He learned early on that if he took long enough to make his move, his opponent would get bored, go to the bathroom, go to sleep or all three. It was said, and nobody could confirm it, but nobody but Petey would deny it, that one player got divorced, moved out of town and returned with a new wife during one of Petey's moves. None of this bothered Petey. Not as long as it gave him a chance to slide checkers around the way he wanted without benefit of rules and regulations. He had adopted the winning is everything philosophy long before Vince Lombardi declared it. And everything to Petey was a 10-cent beer.

On this particular day Petey was especially broke. His wife had worked him over some the night before to get milk money out of him and in a moment of intense pain when she pinned him against the wall with the kitchen table and began flattening his ear with a long-handled skillet, he gave up everything, including the $2.27 he had stashed in a little box of Camay soap he had won at the carnival. There had never been any fear of anyone in his house looking for it there. At any rate, he was in need of a pigeon and he figured he had one when he saw By God Harry Hollis at a table trying to slurp down a bowl of soup. He knew that By God Harry never drank anything without alcohol in it unless he was coming off a long binge and was trying to get back on his feet for the next one.

By God Harry was taking what nourishment his shaking hands would allow him to get to his mouth, but he didn't look good. His face was the color of boiled corn beef and his eyes swam. He was dimly aware of his surroundings, but would have been hard pressed to tell you who or where he was. All he knew was that he was alive and it was not a good feeling at all. Just what Petey was looking for.

"Hey, By God, how are ya?" Petey said, sitting down across from the dissipated hulk. By God Harry tried to look up but found it much too much of an effort and gave up trying. His head hung over the lukewarm bowl of soup.

"How about some checkies?" Petey asked. "Betcha a quart of beer I get all of yours before you get five of mine." Now, this was a shock to the handful of people at the bar who overheard him because Petey never gave anything away to anyone. But Petey figured that By God Harry would barely be able to see the board let alone any slight of hand work that Petey might attempt.

"How bout it, By God, wanna play?" Petey was getting thirsty. The mention of a beer also penetrated By God Harry's alcoholic haze and he slurred, "By God, s'all right with me."

Petey set up the board on the table and pulled the red and black checkers out of his grimy pockets. "You want red or black?" he asked.

"Sure," said By God Harry, starting to come around.

"I mean which one do you want?"

"By God, black. My mother was buried in black", and a tear came to By God Harry's eye.

"Now, don't get no God-damned cryin' jag on," said Petey. "There ain't no room for sentiment in this game." He finished lining up the checkers. "You can have the first move." Another concession that amazed the small crowd that was beginning to pay attention to the proceedings.

By God Harry reached out a shaky hand to make his move, but when he did, he lurched against the small table and sent everything scattering to the floor.

"Damn, By God, sober up. Look what ya done, ya clumsy bastard," complained Petey. But sober up was the last thing Petey wanted because sober By God Harry would not only be able to keep an eye on him, but would also pound Petey into the floor for talking to him that way. Petey scurried around and picked up all the checkers and set up the game again.

This time, By God Harry managed to push his checker forward without destroying everything and the game began. As thirsty as he was, Petey only took about 10 minutes to make his first move, but it was long enough for those at the bar to begin to lose interest and turn back to their own problems.

They weren't too far into the game when By God Harry began to sink back into his alcoholic coma. His head sort of slid over on one arm so that he had a cockeyed view of the table. But his eyes weren't sending any messages to his brain anyway so it didn't really matter. Petey saw that he could now play his kind of game and he slid his chair around to get his back between the checkerboard and the gang at the bar as much as possible. He began to develop his battle plan by sliding his checkers here and By God Harry's checkers there until he had a multiple jump all lined up. By God Harry stared at him and didn't see a thing. "Would you look at this!" Petey said innocently. "You played right into my hands here, By God." And he jumped three of By God Harry's checkers and took them off the board. By God Harry still stared.

"It's your move," Petey said, and By God Harry pawed at another black checker. By now Petey had his magic elbow working and knew he could throw strategy out the window. He had a lock on this game.

Johnny had been observing the grand larceny from behind the bar and a couple of times admonished Petey to keep it honest, knowing that it wouldn't do a damn bit of good. He could see that By God Harry was more interested in a snooze than he was checkers and hollered over to him. "By God, you up to taking solid food yet? I'll fix you a hamburger."

"By God, damned right," By God mumbled.

Johnny went to the kitchen followed by his big mongrel dog Garbage Can, so named because he had the stomach of a billy goat. Johnny never had to put anything out on the curb. Garbage Can consumed it all.

Johnny returned with the hamburger and went behind the bar. "Petey, you want a short beer while By God's eating?" and he set the beer up on the bar.

"Yeah, might's well," said Petey, and he got up and slowly backed over to the bar, keeping an eye on By God Harry to make sure he didn't move the checkers. By God Harry wasn't about to move anything. Johnny carried the hamburger over to By God Harry followed closely by Garbage Can, who was watching diligently for any crumbs that might drop. "Here, By God, this might perk you up," Johnny said as he set the hamburger down. By God Harry began to eat slowly, giving his stomach a chance to adjust to the strange feeling of food. Johnny went back behind the bar followed by Garbage Can and Petey went back to the table and surveyed the checker board. He had By God Harry about whipped already and a couple of slick moves and it was all over.

"Tough break, By God, but you played a helluva game," Petey said triumphantly. By God was stoic in defeat.

"I'm ready for that quart of beer any time you want to buy it," Petey told him. By God Harry stared at him.

Johnny walked over to the table to pick up By God Harry's hamburger plate. He looked at the stack of checkers. "Wait a minute, Petey. What the hell's going on here?" he said, "By God's short a checker. That's not fair."

"The hell he is. He's got the same number I've got," said Petey. "He has not. Look, you got 12 red ones and he's only got 11 black. What kind of a game you playing?"

"No sir," protested Petey. "He had the same number as me. Didn't you, By God?"

By God wasn't hearing either of them much less doing any counting.

"God damn it, Petey, everyone says you cheat, but I didn't know you would handicap a guy by shorting him a checker," Johnny said..

"I didn't, I didn't I tell you," whined Petey, sensing his quart of beer slipping away from him.

"You're the one who brought the checkers in. You're the one who set up the board. No one else has been near the table excepting me and you know damn well I didn't take anything. No sir, all bets are off, and I don't want any more of that kind of nonsense."

"Wait, wait, wait," Petey begged. "It's got to be here someplace, and he dropped on all fours and began crawling around the floor in search of one black checker. Petey spent a frantic half hour feeling his way around the place in his desperate scurry to find his beer ticket.

While he was doing that, Garbage Can was out in the kitchen trying to figure out how he was going to pass that hard lump in his belly without wrecking himself. It was a problem now, but it sure tasted good going down with all that hamburger juice smeared all over it.

HAVE I GOT A DEAL FOR YOU

"I GOT THE BASTARD this time. I really stuck it to him." Gordie Alley was chortling as he strode into The Club with a bulging duffle bag on his back. It was late Saturday afternoon and the bar was full of weekend hopefuls trying to get cranked up. They looked at Gordie with interest because they all knew him and knew he was always up to something.

Gordie was an operator. He could talk his way in and out of hell without getting singed. He'd gotten out of high school after an indifferent performance, had gone into the Army, won the Korean War and had returned home in full uniform wearing every ribbon, medal and badge he could buy in the PX. He paraded around in that outfit for about a week just to make sure he hadn't missed anybody, and he wore bits and pieces of it for months after that as reminders. Today it would be his combat boots, tomorrow his field jacket, the next day his fatigue cap and so on. And he found a campaign ribbon or a good conduct medal pinned to his shirt was always good for a conversation starter.

Gordie was a lanky but rugged sort who wore thick glasses and couldn't be called anything but homely. But that didn't stop him from being about the biggest lady's man around. He had enough bullshit to cover up his gawky appearance and to get sweet young things to believing just about anything he said.

He was always working on a big deal that was going to rake him in a bundle and in the meantime he lived off his mother who dragged down $32 a week working 10 hours a day in the closest thing the town had to a real estate office. It wasn't that Gordie minded work. It was just that he felt overqualified for any of the jobs that his mother was able to scrounge up for him. When he did stoop to menial labor, he made it clear to everyone that it was only temporary until he completed the deal he was working on that would set him up for life. If you were to believe Gordie, he was turning down handsome offers right and left waiting for the one that matched his talents and abilities. In the meantime, he lived out of Mrs. Alley's frayed old pocketbook.

Gordie was a seller and a buyer. He would sell anything in his mother's house that wasn't bolted down and he would buy anything that he didn't already have. He sold and bought guns, TVs, boats, hunting dogs and anything else he could toss in the back of his old pickup truck. He usually owed out more than he had coming in, but that was a cash flow problem that he never worried too much about. If worse came to worse, there was always that old pocketbook.

His sharp eye for a bargain is what put him into a deal with Mallard Dubois. Mallard was to wheeling and dealing what shit was to smell. You didn't get one without the other. Mallard always had something working and it always paid off. And it always meant someone else was going to come up short. When it came to hornswoggling, Mallard was on the top of the heap in the Major Leagues and Gordie was batting around down in Class D ball.

Mallard and Gordie were not a bit alike except for their common interest in making an easy dollar and delighting in seeing the other half of the transaction get stung. Mallard was in his 50s and held a respectable job doing soil tests for the federal government that assured him a fat pension later on. He was a round little man shaped like an egg and he always walked in a big rush with short hurry-up steps.

Mallard's trademark and his key to success was sincerity. He was the most sincere man you ever met. When Mallard started talking to you, you felt as though he had been lying awake all night worrying about you. He would look you straight in the eye with this very concerned expression and say, "Tell me, how the hell are you?" as though he just had to know before he could relax. If you mentioned an ailment, he would say, "You don't say. That's a real shame. A real shame. I'm sorry to hear that, I really am," and so on.

Mallard wasn't a bit concerned about your health, not unless he thought you were dying and were going to leave something he hadn't been able to lay claim to, something that he could hawk at the auction barn. The auction barn was Mallard's base of operation. It was there he turned sincerity into a profitable enterprise. It was a big old two-story barn that had originally been built to keep horses, had later been turned into a car repair shop and in recent years had been reworked to accommodate the auction held every Saturday beginning in mid-afternoon. The auction was the biggest social event in town. Mill Town had its Granges and Rotarys and Women's Guilds and Civic Clubs and all that for those who needed them, but they naturally were members-only kind of things. The auction was for everybody. There was something for the entire family. Kids could pet the calves, sheep and ponies and lust for the repainted two-wheeler with the basket on the front and the wagon hitch on the back that was wearing an out-of-sight $4 price tag on the handlebars. Teenage girls and boys could stroll around in their best non-Sunday clothes pretending not to notice each other.

Wives and mothers could sit around and chat about things they had sat around and chatted about last week, always with an eye out for a second-hand egg beater or some other recycled gadget that would make their domestic bliss a little more blissful.

The men could climb up on the rough plank seats and look over the cattle or lawnmowers or young women who reminded them of what their wives once looked like, all the while keeping an eye out for the dirty joke conspiracy and hoping they could get in on it.

Mallard was the initiator of the dirty joke conspiracy and early on in the auction when canning jars or oil cloth samples were on the block he would furtively motion to a select few men to join him out in the back of the barn where the animals were kept and where the women wouldn't stray for fear of picking up the barn smells on their Saturday clothes.

After making sure he hadn't gotten any seriously practicing Baptists into the group, Mallard would giggle out the best dirty jokes he had heard on his rounds that week. It was a great feeling to be included in the joke-telling group, and it was also another of Mallard's ways of setting up his pigeon. There were certain men-about-town who were always included and each week Mallard would include a couple of less sophisticated types who seldom get included in anything except March of Dime fund drives. They would feel an enormous debt of gratitude to Mallard and the uneasy trust two conspirators must have to have a conspiracy. Mallard wouldn't do a job on someone he had personally selected to share in this sworn-to-silence ritual , now would he? You bet your sweet ass he would. He had a voracious eye for the soft underbelly.

Gordie Alley had long since been gestured into the conspiracy and had gone on to gather his own audience, but it was mostly the younger guys who didn't have that much worth sweating out a scam on. Gordie was a born actor and a much better joke teller than Mallard, but an invitation from Gordie just didn't carry the status of a Mallard nod.

The two had matched their devious wits a number of times and Gordie had always come out on the short end of things. There was the time Mallard sold Gordie the sure-fire, guaranteed, natural- born, rabbit -hunting beagle hound. It wasn't until the animal had sneezed its way across three fields that George found out it had some rare kind of dog asthma and couldn't smell a thing. And then there was the time Mallard had casually asked Gordie about an old rocker he said he had let Gordie's granddad have years before for a couple of bucks and that he would like to get back for sentimental reasons.

Gordie let it go for $10 and found out later that it was a genuine Shaker piece that Mallard got fixed up and sold to an antique dealer for $450. These and a good many other deals gone sour were in the front of Gordie's mind when he stopped in the auction barn and saw the bulging duffle bag with the ball glove sticking out of the top.

Gordie had been a fair pitcher for the high school team and took an immediate interest. The glove on top was a brand new catcher's mitt, Major League quality. George looked it over for a minute and peeked into the duffle bag and saw it was full of baseball gloves, all apparently of the same quality.

"Where'd these ball gloves come from?" he asked Mallard, who was busy putting price tags on auction items.

"Oh, I got those from a sporting goods guy on his way through to Binghamton. His radiator blew just outside of town and I traded him a second-hand one for that bag of sporting good stuff there. I don't know a damn thing about it, but he said it was top caliber stuff. Said the pros use it."

"Well, I wouldn't say it was all that good, but it looks usable," Gordie said casually. "I been thinking of getting a Little League team together. You know. Give the kids somethin' to do. I don't mind donating my time, but I can't go outfitting the whole team. Most of the kids in this town don't have anything but rags for gloves. What do you think you're going to be asking for those?"

"Hell, I don't know. I never played ball. You know more about it than I do. Anything that's fair is OK with me."

"Bein's I'm going to be handing them over to the kids, I can't afford to go too high. How's about one price for the whole bag?" "Tell you what I'll do, Gordie. As long as it's for the kids, I'm willing to take a little whack on the deal myself. What's a fair price for the works?"

"I'd say $10 is about right."

"$30."

"$30? Good God, Mallard, I can't go that high. I haven't even got the team together yet. I'll go $15, but that's it."

"Gordie, that radiator was worth $30," Mallard complained. "But I'm not going to stand in the way of a ball team for this town. You can have the kit and caboodle for $20 and that's stealing them." "$20? I wouldn't call it stealin', but I guess I can see $20," and Gordie pulled the money from his wallet.

He shouldered the duffle bag and headed for his pickup doing everything he could to hide his excitement. He laid the bag carefully in the back, jumped in the front and took off.

"Hot damn! I did it this time! I got him!" Gordie could barely contain himself as he drove up the street. "There's got to be a dozen gloves in there and I'll get $20 bucks apiece for every one of them. I can't believe Mallard bought that shit about a Little League team. Wait till he finds out what these things are worth. He'll piss vinegar."

Gordie had to tell somebody. You didn't get Mallard every day. He headed straight for The Club.

His declaration of triumph over Mallard when he walked into the bar stirred considerable interest and the crowd listened with delight as Gordie went into a drawn out account of how he slickered the slickest one of them all.

"That looks like a real good glove, Gordie," said Donkey Nuts. "Let me see it."

"Sure," Gordie said. "Everyone of these is worth at least $30-$40." Others wanted to take a look so Donkey Nuts began dealing out gloves from the bag. Soon a dozen guys were sitting at the bar with ball gloves on their hands.

"When he said he was going to give me a break because of the kids, it was all I could do to keep from laughing in his face," Gordie continued. "He said $30 for the works and that would have been just about giving them away, but I pretended it was outrageous and knocked him down to $20."

"This sure is good leather, all right," said Donkey Nuts, "but this here's a catcher's mitt."

"So? They're worth more than a fielder's glove."

"Yeah, but this is a left-handed mitt. I ain't never seen a left-handed catcher."

"The one I got is a left-handed catcher's mitt, too," said Willard Klemp, thumping the pocket.

"So's this one," said Glenn Tink.

"Yeah, this here's a left-handed mitt," and so on down the bar as Gordie's expression changed from delight to puzzlement to seething rage. He spent the rest of the afternoon getting drunk to the derisive laughter as he set up his strategy for getting rid of a dozen grade A, top flight, Major League-quality left-handed catcher's mitts.

JUST A LITTLE LOVIN'

"I'M SO HORNY I can just about walk," lamented Sammy Griney as he knocked down a beer on a slow afternoon in May. "Wish the hell it was carnival time so I could do some good for myself." Sammy was musing mostly to himself with Gordie Alley, Donkey Nuts, Glenn Tink, Clancy Riordin and Johnny listening in. It was one of those days when everyone had been rained out of work late enough in the day not to start some inside job, but early enough not to go home.

"You're not goin' to see no carnival for more'n a month," said Donkey Nuts. "Your old coconuts are gonna shrivel right up into raisins by then."

"They're hard as coconuts all right," moaned Sammy. "I gotta' walk bowlegged to keep from hurtin' myself. Damn, I could use some action."

As a matter of fact, when it came to women, Sammy would have made a good priest. That's how much action he got. About the only woman he ever got close to was Peg Cavanaugh and that was when she wrestled his struggling little form out on to the dance floor.

His sexual encounters were pretty much limited to once-a-year gropes with the women from the girlie shows in the carnivals that set up shop in a field just outside of town for two- or three-day stands. Anyone with the right amount of change in his pocket could pay the girls a visit after the show and Sammy was always one of the first in line.

They usually talked him out of twice as much as he was figuring on spending by telling him what a super stud he was. He rationalized the expense by telling himself that, if he could find a woman who would go out with him, which was unlikely, and if he was going to make any time with her, which was even more unlikely, he was going to have to buy her flowers, candy, a few beers and even take her out for eats once in awhile, and that would set him back plenty with no guarantee that he would even get his finger wet. So when you got right down to it, paying the carnival girls a few extra bucks was smart finance.

The only problem was that the carnival girls only showed up a couple of times during the summer and Sammy had the hard rocks all year around. He was just over 40 and had read somewhere that men reached their sexual peak at 18. Sammy hadn't had a peek at anything at 18 and even at 40 still hadn't had what you would call a good look. He could see his sex life slipping away on him and it worried him plenty.

"What you need, my lad, is a respectable woman who you can flop down anytime you want to," said Clancy, "Somebody who'll look out for your creature needs without demanding all kinds of fringe benefits."

"Hell, that's what we all need," said Donkey Nuts. "I'm handin' out all them fringe benefits you're talkin' about and I'm not doin' much better than Sammy and I've been married for 12 years."

Clancy, A soft-voiced little Irish carpenter with a plump, pleasant grandmotherly wife and two grown kids, never got too involved with the emotional or romantic ups and downs of the other Club members. He liked to come in a couple of times a week, drink too much beer, listen to all the lies, laugh at the jokes and then go home to all the repair jobs his wife kept coming up with. He liked coming into The Club just often enough and long enough so that he was expected there without being greeted like a stranger or guest. He preferred the comfortable nods he would get to the back-slapping greetings reserved for someone who was only an occasional visitor. He stopped in often enough to keep his dues paid up and that was all he wanted.

He had a wry, straight-faced sense of humor that often went unappreciated partly because it was so subtle and partly because he spoke so quietly that no one could hear him. You really had to pay attention to Clancy if you wanted to know what he was saying. As often as not, his observations were lost in the raucous chatter around him.

"I don't know no respectable women," Sammy wailed. "Least none that will go out with me. There ain't a woman in this town that'd be caught dead with me."

Sammy had a point. In addition to being little more than bar stool-tall, he had a red, rawhide face that had rough times written all over it. His teeth had long since left him for a variety of reasons and the tobacco he chewed left a brown ring around his mouth that seemed to have stained into his skin. He kept relatively clean but had a limited wardrobe of levis and checkered flannel shirts so he wasn't able to change every day.

But he had a good soul and everybody liked him. He would do anything for anybody, no questions asked, and no favors asked in return. He was good for a loan when he had it and when he didn't, he would help you get it from someone else. He had tried numerous times to get himself a steady companion, but, despite his good nature and generosity, he couldn't find any takers. Women didn't mind sharing a beer or a laugh with Sammy, but they just weren't a bit excited about bedding down with him. So when Clancy suggested he find a respectable woman, the boys at the bar knew it was more dry humor than it was a serious proposal. But Clancy continued.

"I wouldn't give up if I was you," he said. "I'm doing some porch work for Miss DeSimmons down at the edge of town and she's got some shirttail relative from Chicago come to stay with her for awhile. A fourth cousin or something like that. She's a fair looker, too. Can't be more than 50-55. She leans a little bit toward fat and she lays on the makeup pretty thick, but all in all, she's presentable."

"The main thing is she's friendly. She was gushin' all over me when I met her and she was saying how she always wanted to live in a small town because the people were so friendly and how cold and hardboiled people are in Chicago. She made a big point about how she wanted to get to know people here. No reason why you can't be one of the first, Sammy."

"Are you kiddin'? If she's presentable, she ain't goin' to have nothing to do with me."

"Naw, I don't mean she's fancy or anything. She's not. Fact, most of the women around here won't go for all that makeup and all the trinkets she wears. She wears that shiny stuff around her eyes and I think she even wears those false eye lashes. But, what the hell, she's from Chicago."

"Yeah, women around here don't know nothin' about dressin', anyway." Sammy was beginning to get interested. He knew it was a long shot, but his opportunities were few and far between. He couldn't afford to pass up anything.

"How do I get a look at her? I'd at least like to check her out and see if she's my type." That drew a roll of laughter down the bar. "No, I mean it," Sammy protested. "We might not be what'cha call it, compatible." More laughter.

"All you got to do is stop by when I'm working down there and pretend you've got to see me about something. She's bound to be around and I'll make the intros," said Clancy.

"OK, I'll stop by about quittin' time tomorrow and if it works out, I'll buy you a beer," Sammy promised.

The next afternoon Clancy and Sammy walked into The Club. That is, Clancy walked in. Sammy pranced. He could barely contain himself.

"A beer for Clancy here, Johnny. All the beer he wants, By God."

"Well, looks like things went pretty well," said Johnny. "Pretty well? You better believe pretty well," said Sammy. "I never had to ask her nothin'. She asked me to take her out sometime. You believe that? She asked me."

"What the hell are you talking about?" asked Johnny, looking over at Clancy.

"It's true," Clancy said quietly. "She asked him out."

"She must be some dog ugly if she asked you out," said Gordie Alley.

"She ain't. She ain't a bit," Sammy squeaked. "She's a fine lookin' woman. She's gorgeous."

"Now, wait a minute, Sammy, she's not that sharp," cautioned Clancy. "She wears an awful lot of makeup."

"So what, she's from Chicago, right? What do you expect? They're used to dressin' up more, that's all."

"What I want to know is how the hell she came to ask you out," said Johnny.

"I dunno. I stopped down like Clancy said and pretended I had to borrow some tools and while we was talkin', she came out onto the porch and asked if we was thirsty. Clancy told her my name and we right away get talkin' about things, she askin' me what I did and was I married and what did I do for fun and all that. I told her I liked to go to stock car races and she got all excited and said she had never seen one, but always wondered what they was like. Then she asked me would I mind takin' her sometime. I couldn't hardly believe it. She was askin' me."

"He damn near pissed his pants," Clancy said.

"I did not, I just wasn't expectin' it."

Johnny wasn't expecting it either. Nor were any of the other Club members who sat there in disbelief. Johnny said, "Are you shitting me Clancy? Are you guys making this up?"

"No, it's like he said. She just asked him, casual as anything."

"Well, Sammy, I've got to hand it to you," said Johnny. "Looks like you've got yourself a girlfriend."

"I wouldn 't go so far as to say that," Sammy replied. "It's awful early to say that. But we did hit it right off. She was interested in everything I brought up. I told her about drivin' truck over at the mill and she thought that was great. And I told her about goin' to the auction on Saturdays and she thought that was great, too. She said it sounded to her like life in Mill Town is a lot of fun. I never much thought of it that way but, you know, if you look at it from the big city angle, maybe it is."

"Mill Town is about as much fun as sittin' in a dentist's office," said Donkey Nuts.

"See, that's your problem. You don't know how to appreciate things. You don't know what you got."

"You never thought it was so hot yourself," said Donkey Nuts.

"That's 'cause I never looked at it the way she does. She looks on the fun side of things. She's got good perspective."

"Well, I hope she's got one good thing or you're goin' to be wastin' a lot of time and money," said Donkey Nuts sourly and that got everyone going.

"He's right, Sammy," said Gordie Alley. "All the fun you want is right in the back seat of your old 1949 Chevy."

"Yeah, it's about time you baptized that thing," snickered Glenn Tink.

"Now, cut that out!" Sammy was getting annoyed. "That's all you guys ever talk about. It ain't right to talk about her like that. Just 'cause she's got some class, don't give you the right to make fun of her. You guys could use some."

"I could use some, all right, but it ain't class. Sounds a lot like it, though," snorted Donkey Nuts.

That really brought the house down and it brought Sammy up. "Goddamnit," he said, standing on the rung of a barstool. "You cut that out. You got no call to talk like that. You ain't even met her."

"All right, Sammy, just calm down," said Johnny. "Donk is just having some fun. When are we going to meet her, anyway?"

"I'm not sure I want to bring her in here. I can't trust you guys. You'll go and say something and ruin everything."

"Don't worry, nobody's going to say anything. I'll make sure of that," Johnny said. He turned to the slurpers. "The first one to say anything out of line is shut off for a month." A double-barreled shotgun aimed right between their eyes would not have had more effect on them. Sammy had reason to fear no longer. "We're goin' to the stock car races tomorrow night," he said. "I told her about this place and she said she wanted to meet everbody so I said we'd stop on the way to the races. But I ain't going to bring her in here and get her insulted."

"I told you not to worry," said Johnny. And Sammy wasn't really worried that much after hearing Johnny's chilling edict. It even frightened him.

"OK, I'll bring her in." Then he motioned Johnny down to the other end of the bar. "I got to get somethin' decent to wear. What do you think I would look good in?"

Johnny was much too nice a guy to answer that question honestly so he just said, "Hell, I don't know. Just about anything would be all right, I guess. You're going to the races so you don't want to get too dressed up."

Dressing up for Sammy was to search through the pile on his bedroom floor and find the shirt with the least amount of sawdust on it, shake it out and put it on. He also was particularly proud of a pair of shiny patent leather semi-cowboy boots with zippers up the insides. He painfully ignored the fact they were a full size too small for him. They had very high heels and he felt they made him look considerably taller.

They became known in The Club as Sammy's fairy boots because it hurt him so much to walk in them that he had to sort of tip toe along in them. When he wore them, which was not too often, he would mince his way to the end of the bar nearest the bathroom and then stay there for the night.

He had long since managed to ignore the homosexual references to his footwear and could even join in the fun when one of the guys would ask him for a date.

But now, dressing was serious business. "I'm goin' over to the department store and get some things," he told Johnny. "I just don't know what to pick out."

"What kind of things?" Johnny asked.

"Some shirts and pants and some underwear, maybe some new socks."

"Where are you going to get the money for that? I can help you out some if you like. Just pay me back when you can."

"Naw, I'm all right there. Mrs. Haynes lets me run a bill." What he didn't tell Johnny is that Mrs. Haynes, who ran the little one-suit store, was also sworn to secrecy not to tell anyone that Sammy had to shop in the boy's section. She had honored the promise and would even have Sammy stand in the men's section while she unobtrusively brought his clothes from the boy's section to look at.

"Get whatever you feel good in," Johnny said. "That's the best way to buy clothes."

"Yeah, you're right. That's what I'll do."

The next day was Saturday and by mid-afternoon the word about Sammy's date had reached just about anyone who would be interested and The Club began to fill up. Johnny admonished each member as he poured him his first drink that there was to be no smart remarks. Sammy was to be the king, they were the subjects and his lady friend the visiting queen. They were to act accordingly.

Conversations turned to other things as they waited and The Club took on its usual Saturday afternoon clatter. By God Harry Hollis was working hard on keeping the third day of a four-day binge going and Dana Grimes was trying to blot out the realization that sooner or later he was going to have to drag himself back to that dreary wife of his.

"Sammy's here!"

Everybody shut up and turned toward the door. Even the juke box discarded its last record. Silence.

"C'mon, act natural," Johnny said. "You're going to make him feel funny."

It didn't do any good. They had all waited too long to get a look at Sammy's big opportunity to miss out on it now. The door opened and Sammy stepped in with his date.

Any scrutiny, inspection or consideration of the lady on his arm was momentarily forgotten as Club members stared at the little man. Sammy Griney had got slicked up. He had got so slicked up he shined from the top of his balding head to the tips of his patent leather boots. He stood there in an explosion of colors that fought each other tooth and nail. He wore a mint green sport jacket over a blue plaid flannel shirt that was slit down the middle by a blinding yellow necktie that reached almost all the way across his middle. Below that were a pair of orange-purple-blue-green plaid slacks that were secured in front with an almost-new 1954 Calgary Stampede rodeo belt buckle big enough to fry a 14-ounce steak on. His patent leather boots sparkled almost as much as did Sammy himself. He was well-scrubbed and his sun-reddened face shone all the way up to the hat line where it turned white and continued to the back of his head.

Johnny had not needed to worry about ungracious comments. The Club members were speechless. They just stared at this stranger in front of them. They barely noticed the smiling woman on his arm. Willard Klemp finally found words.

"Jesus Christ, Sammy, where did you find that getup?"

"What do you mean? These were just some things I had hangin' in the closet." Sammy was still a little nervous and he didn't want his romantic interest to know that he had had to go out and buy all new clothes just to go out on a date, and to the stock car races at that. He especially didn't want anyone to know that it was the only combination of clothes Mrs. Haynes had in a boy's size that would fit him. She had tried hard to dissuade him from buying them, but Sammy figured any new clothes were better than none at all so he charged the whole package.

As Club members' eyes became adjusted to the clashing colors shouting at them, they turned to the original object of their attention – Sammy's date.

Under any other circumstances she would have stolen the fashion show herself. Club members were looking at a woman in her late 40s to mid-50s, depending on who was guessing, who had taken pains to fill in the beginning wrinkles carefully with pancake makeup on a pleasant, slightly pudgy face that once had been pretty. Her eyes were clear and warm behind more mascara and pencil makeup than most women in town would have used in a year. The makeup and turned-up eyelashes were meticulously applied and had a striking effect. But no more striking than her hair which was a silver-blonde done up in a beehive the texture of cotton candy. It had obviously taken hours to prepare and it was also obvious that only the hairdresser would know how much of it was real silver and how much was the hairdresser's handiwork.

A pair of long sparkling earrings pointed down to a bright red fuzzy waist length coat covering a fluorescent blue silky dress that was cut full to hide the extra pounds that age had placed around her hips. She was full-breasted and they carried a large three-string necklace that dipped into their cleavage. She was wearing black stockings, something not often seen on the women in town, and they covered a pair of legs a much younger woman would envy. She wore a pair of black shoes that were almost as shiny as Sammy's and with high heels that clicked when she walked. They also brought her up to eye level with Sammy.

Sammy wasn't quite sure where to start the introductions so he took her by the elbow and led her over to the bar.

"Johnny, meet May Farley."

"Well, how do you do, ma'am. Very pleased to meet you," said Johnny warmly. "Sammy's told us a lot about you and we've been hoping we'd get a chance to meet you."

"Very pleased to meet you, Johnny. Sammy's told me so many nice things about his friends here, I just had to stop by and see for myself."

"Yeah, Well, Sammy's always been something of a bullshitter," snorted Gordie Alley.

"Hey, watch your language," growled Donkey Nuts menacingly low enough that May couldn't hear him, but loud enough to put the fear of God into Gordie.

One by one, Sammy introduced May to the customers, stopping for a moment at each barstool to exchange names. Most of them, despite their earlier snide remarks and teasing, became awkward and uneasy when actually confronted with a strange woman. They mumbled hello or just ma'am and didn't know what else to say.

Gordie Alley, on the other hand, had never been at a loss for words and this was no exception. "Pleased to make your acquaintance, ma'am," he drawled as he slipped quickly into his favorite role of the unsophisticated farm boy. "We're right proud you saw fit to drop in on us like this. It ain't often we get to meet someone from the city, especially someone so pretty."

Sammy began to get uneasy. He had seen Gordie put people on too many times with his ah, shucks, country boy routine.

"Well, thank you, sir. I can see your lack of education hasn't stunted you on manners any," replied May with a sweet smile that told Gordie she could play his game all day long. Gordie decided it best to lay off. Sammy beamed. "You got time for a drink before you go to the track, Sammy?" Johnny asked.

"Yeah, sure, we got lots of time. What kind of beer do you want, May?"

"Oh, I don't really care for beer. I'd just as soon have a glass of chilled white wine if that would be possible."

"Wine? Heck, we've got to have some wine here somewhere," said Johnny as he rummaged around under the bar. He came up with a bottle with a screw cap and opened it. "I'm afraid it's not chilled, but I can put some ice in it."

"That would be just fine," May said. "I don't mean to be a bother."

"Oh, it's no bother," Johnny said. "I just forgot to put it in the cooler. Sammy says you're here from Chicago."

"Yes, I've lived most of my life there," May said as Sammy seated her on a barstool. She surveyed the group at the bar, smiling slightly each time she made eye contact. "It's much quieter here. You get tired of all that noise and traffic. There is much more to do there, of course, but I think this is a beautiful little town."

"Yes, it is. The pace is a little slow, but it's a nice place to live. There's security in a small town like this. People have to help you whether they want to or not," said Johnny, "It's expected of you."

"I think that's wonderful. Everybody helping everybody. You don't see much of that in the city," May said. "Everybody's looking out for themselves."

"You get some of that here, too," Johnny replied, "but not all that much. We all know each other so it's pretty hard to turn your back on someone."

"Well, I'm hoping to get to know all of you real well, myself," said May warmly. "Sammy said he has a lot of nice friends and I can see he's right." Sammy slipped off the barstool. "Well, we hate to run, But we better get goin' or we're goin' to miss the first race. Maybe we'll stop on the way back if it's not too late."

"Why, Sammy, you think I'm going to turn into a pumpkin or something? Of course we'll stop," May said, smiling.

Sammy hesitantly took her arm. This was new business to him and he wasn't sure quite how to go about it so he gripped her left bicep and steered her toward the door. May gently removed his hand and slipped her arm through his. The evaluations began as soon as the door closed behind them.

"Where the hell did Sammy get a hold of something like that?" Glenn Tink wanted to know. "She's not a bad looker at all." "You're tellin' me," said Willard Klemp. "I wouldn't mind taking a crack at that my own self."

"Willard, you'd take a crack at a milk snake," Gordie Alley said, "but you're right, she's pretty sharp even if she does have sort of a smart ass tongue on her."

After all the comments were exchanged, the consensus was that May Farley was an uncommonly attractive woman with a lot of good miles left on her. She showed some signs of wear and tear but by and large had weathered her years quite well. But why was she going out with Sammy? Little squeaky-voiced, no-teeth, sawmill-raw Sammy? He was their friend and anything they had was his, but that didn't overlook the fact that Sammy was no lady killer. Maybe she saw the qualities they all knew were there but did not bother to dwell on. At any rate, despite some minor pangs of envy, they were all pleased to see their little friend doing so well for himself.

There were still some occasional remarks about the couple as Saturday pushed its way toward midnight and Club members relentlessly stepped up their pursuit of the evening's perfect moment.

Johnny kept pouring warmth and his patrons consumed it with ever-widening smiles of gratitude. Sunday morning was eons away and maybe for once it wouldn't ever get here.

This pleasant thought was going through several minds when the door flew open and Sammy burst in. He slammed the door behind him and stomped to the bar in his patent leather boots. He was beside himself.

"Goddamned son-of-a-bitch anyway. Would you believe that? I can't believe it. I just can't Goddamn believe it."

"What the hell's eating you, Sammy?" Johnny asked. "What's got your ass in an uproar?"

"It ain't right, Johnny. It just ain't right. I finally got myself a woman and what happens? It just ain't fair."

"What isn't fair? What the hell are you talking about?"

"And on top of all that I go way into hock to get these fancy clothes and spend damn near every cent I've made for a month and now this."

"What is it? What happened?"

"You're not goin' to believe this. We got to the track, right? We're havin' a great time, we're talkin', we get somethin' to eat, we watch the races, everything's fine. After the races are over, I start for home. She moves over real close to me on the seat and says, 'Why don't we stop somewhere?' I figured she wanted to get somethin' to eat and I was runnin' short of cash, but I figured I might as well go for it, so I asked her if she wanted a hamburger or somethin'. She said no, she meant let's stop somewhere quiet where we could talk. And then she puts her hand on my leg. I'm not shittin', just like that without my sayin' a word. You believe that? Right on my leg and way high up, too.

"I wasn't about to lose out on this so I head right down behind the old viaduct and parked. I didn't hardly get the key shut off before we was smoochin' like crazy. I swear she was climbin' all over me. She helped me get her brassiere unhooked and everything. We were gettin' down to serious business when she starts tellin' me how she likes me a lot and all but how she is all alone and has to look out for herself and how she hasn't got much to get by on and did I think it was worth fifty bucks to keep on goin' with what we were doin'. Fifty bucks! You believe that! Fifty bucks! She was chargin' me!" Sammy's indignation had raised his voice to an enraged squeak. He was beside himself.

"And then you know what she said? She said maybe I could get her better acquainted with some of the other guys in here bein's I was friends with everybody. I do her a favor and she'd do me a favor. You believe that! She wanted me to be a Goddamned pimp!"

"God, Sammy, I'm sorry," Johnny said, trying desperately to keep from cracking up at the sight of the angry little man stamping his patent leather boots. "I never would have guessed her to be that kind. Well, you're well rid of her. You were right to kick her ass out."

"What are you talkin about?" Sammy answered impatiently. "I got her out in the car. I told you I was runnin' short. I only got 15 bucks left and I wondered if you could let me have $35 till the first of the month."

SO WHO WANTS THE PULITZER?

"IF THE DAY AIN'T hazy, the dog ain't lazy."

"Now, what the hell is that supposed to mean, Roy?" asked Donkey Nuts.

"I don't explain 'em. I just make em' up," replied Rhymin' Roy Williams with a smug smile.

"But that don't mean anything," continued Donkey Nuts. "What's a lazy dog got to do with a day that ain't hazy?"

"You'll have to figure that out for yourself," said Roy, and that was as far as he was going to go. Roy never explained his rhymes. He just dropped them on the bar once in awhile and let everyone else figure out what to do with them. And most of the time they ended up fighting and arguing about what they meant or if they meant anything or if Roy even had an idea what they meant. Rhymin' Roy was not about to jeopardize his status as poet laureate of The Club by trying to explain his work. The way Roy looked at it, if it rhymed it was a poem and that ought to be enough. It was hard enough to get them to rhyme without having them make sense.

Rhymin' Roy drove hay truck for a living and spent many hours on the road alone and, apart from damn near killing himself trying to catch a look at women's legs in cars passing him, he found the work got boring real fast. He didn't mind the summer driving so much because it was then that some women would hike their dresses up a little to cool off and when they would pass him he could look down and get a delightful view.

If he saw one with a fair amount of thigh showing, he would put the pedal to the floor and try to stay as close behind as he could until he came to a downhill stretch. He would then open it up all the way and let the weight of his top-heavy load push him past the car he was zeroing in on. He would go barreling down the hill with his load swaying back and forth, praying that nothing would be coming up the hill the other way. He'd pass the car, get back into the right hand lane and slow down. Sooner or later, his quarry would get tired of sitting behind the old hay truck, not being able to see around it, especially if Roy slowed to 30 mph as he often did. He would stop in the middle of the road if that was what it would take to get her to pass.

So the object of his ogling would attempt to pass, and Roy would crank it up again to try to keep her right along side of him for as long as he could and a longer shot of her legs and whatever else he could see. Most of the time they caught on to him within a few seconds and would speed away, leaving Roy trying to lock the view into his memory for future reference.

Roy's greatest moment came one day when he was sailing down the three lane to Scranton and a convertible carrying two young women started to pass. As they got along side, Roy began sighting in the way a bombardier does as he approaches the target. As they crept close, his eyes locked in on the front seat and that was when he just about lost it all together. He was staring into two bare crotches! The women had their dresses hiked up around their waists and neither of them was wearing panties.

Roy was so shocked he forgot what he was doing for a minute until he felt the truck begin to bump and buck and he realized he'd run off onto the shoulder of the road. He was fighting to get control of the truck when he saw the two women throw their heads back and laugh uproariously as they stepped on it and sped away. He wound his old 1948 Mack up until it was screaming at him, but he didn't have a prayer of catching them. He finally backed off, but he spent the rest of his trip checking every diner and gas station along Route 11 looking for their car.

He knew no one in The Club would believe his story no matter how graphically and explicitly he related it. By the time he had made it back from Scranton, and after having reviewed the incident dozens of times in his mind – he even squeezed his eyes shut so he could picture it better – he decided that both of the women had been beautiful, one was a redhead and the other a blonde and they both had been smiling at him, giving him the come-on. They had also signaled him that they wanted some company, but he got stuck in traffic and missed where they turned off. By the time he walked into The Club, he had gone over it so many times that he had convinced himself it was true.

But he wasn't convincing anyone in The Club.

"Bullshit, Roy," Donkey Nuts snorted, after Roy had spent a half hour stretching every detail he could for the half dozen Club regulars at the bar. "You got more shit than a barnyard."

"I swear to ya, it's true," said Roy. "They pulled right up there and flashed those things just surer than hell."

"Tell us again, now, you say they just sat there with the top down and everything?" said Glenn Tink. He and everyone else in the bar were doubtful of Roy's story, but they wanted very much to be able to believe him. If it had happened to Roy, it could happen to them.

"I'm tellin' ya, I'm just sittin' there listenin' to Hank Williams when this red convertible commences to come along side real slow. That's what got me to lookin'. They was comin' up real careful and takin' their time. They gets up along side and the one on my side gives me this big smile and nods at me. By then they're not tryin' to pass or nothin'. They're just cruisin' there. I can tell they're interested by the way the one was givin' me this real hot look. She's practically tellin' me to pull over."

"OK, but when did you see they weren't wearin' anything?" asked Gordie Alley. By now they all were crowded around the corner of the bar where Roy sat with their heads leaned in toward him so they wouldn't miss a word.

"Well, like I said, this one gives me the real come-on. I mean, you can tell she's lookin' for somethin'! They still wasn't quite even with me, so all I could see was these two big smiles, but I'm tellin' ya, they was gorgeous. They couldn't either one of them been more than 30."

"God damn it, Roy, let's hear about the beaver," said Willard Klemp impatiently.

"Yeah, right, well, I'm smilin' right back at 'em when the blonde steps on it a little and pulls up a little farther. About then I looks ahead to make sure I don't kill my damn self and then I turn back to the car. Wham! There it is! Right in front of me. You can almost see all the way up to their bellybuttons. I mean they was right there bare ass."

By this time everyone in The Club was driving right down the road with Pete. They were all sitting in that driver's seat staring into the convertible.

"My God, sort of restores your faith in mankind, don't it?" said Willard after a moment of silence as each of them tried to make the scene as real as they could.

"It sure as hell does," said Donkey Nuts. "I been runnin' that three-lane for a long time just hopin' somethin' like that would happen to me. It gives you somethin' to look forward to."

"I'll tell you one thing you can put in your hip pocket," said Gordie Alley. "If it was me, they would never have got lost in traffic. I would have run every son of a bitch in Pennsylvania off the road before I would have let them get lost."

"Sure, Gordie, and some day you're going to get the best of Mallard," said Johnny, and everyone roared.

"Well, all I can say," said Roy, trying to keep from losing his audience to Gordie's ribbing, "is that you can't shave a beaver with an old dull cleaver."

"Hey, that's not bad, Roy," said Gordie, who didn't mind changing the subject about his bouts with Mallard. "That's got kind of a ring to it.."

"Yeah, but it don't mean a God-damned thing," said Donkey Nuts, "What good's a poem that don't mean anything?"

"They don't have to mean anything," said Roy. "When I was in school, I read lots of poems that didn't mean anything, but they was still pretty."

"Roy's right, Some of the most famous ones don't make any sense at all," said Gordie. "The words are just sort of all scrambled up. I've seen books with lots of 'em in it that don't even rhyme, and they're considered to be great."

"I'm no literature expert, mind ya', but I like them to rhyme," said Willard. "I like the ones that hop right along with a nice beat to them. My favorite is the one about The Cremation of Sam McGee. Now that thing rhymes all the way through."

"Well now, I know that one," said Gordie, stepping away from the bar to take center stage as he was inclined to do whenever he assumed his theatrical role. "There are strange things done in the midnight sun..." he began dramatically.

"Cut the shit, Gordie," said Donkey Nuts before he could get warmed up. "I like the one about 'There was an old lady … ' there's a whole bunch of them."

Gordie wasn't a bit happy about Donkey Nuts closing the curtain on his performance and he had some thoughts of calling him on it, but he could see that Donkey Nuts didn't even realize he had been rude and Gordie wasn't about to risk stirring the Donk up over a poem he wasn't even sure he could remember all the way through.

Johnny could see the beginning of the most intense literary discussion carried on in The Club since the cold meat salesman had left off that booklet of Burma Shave sign jingles several months back and he decided to make the most of it.

"You guys think what Roy does is easy? Well, I say it takes a real ear. It's something you're born with, raw talent so to speak. I'm going to give all of you a chance to write a poem and just see how they match up to Roy's. You can write about anything you want to and as long as you want. You don't have to keep them just to one line the way Roy does."

He went out into the kitchen and came back with a large tablet and a handful of assorted pencils. He gave each of them a sheet of the tablet paper and a pencil. "We won't rush this, gentlemen, great writing can't be hurried. You all have until 3 o'clock to finish your work. That's more than two hours and plenty of time to write a poem," Johnny said.

"Shit, I'm not going to waste my time wracking my brain over somethin' like that. It's all I can do to make out a grocery list," Glenn Tink said as he pushed the sheet of paper back across the bar.

"I neglected to mention that the winner of this poetry contest gets a quart of beer and a pickled sausage," said Johnny. Tink quickly retrieved his piece of paper and By God Harry Hollis, who had taken little interest in the literary discussion up to that point, having been too busy trying to convince himself that the top of Johnny's mahogany bar was actually a soft, down pillow, raised his head and said, "By God, gimme a pencil." Even Starley Basil, who hadn't written so much as his name on anything in years, accepted a paper and pencil,.

For awhile, the conversation stopped as each of the contestants bent his head to his work. The only sound was an occasional murmer as one of them mumbled a phrase or a line to himself to test it before putting it on paper. It was a strange sight for The Club, a row of hard-working, hard-drinking blue collar toilers with their heads down hunkered over pieces of paper and their faces pained and contorted in the agony of original thought.

By God Harry had surrounded his paper with a massive left arm to prevent anyone from copying off him and the strain of his concentration forced the end of his tongue out the right corner of his mouth. The stub of a pencil he held was lost in his meaty hand and it looked as if he was writing with the ends of his work-stained fingers. It was first grade all over for By God Harry, as he slowly squeezed out the words that came so hard.

"Damn, I need a break," Gordie Alley said as he raised his head and stretched back. "Give me a beer, Johnny, I can't concentrate unless I 'm relaxed."

Donkey Nuts also looked up. "Yeah, give me one, too. This is tense work."

The others put down their pencils and agreed that you couldn't expect a person to just keep on writing forever without something to keep him going. Normal conversation returned to the bar except for the occasional moment of inspiration when one of them would quickly jot down a few words. Only Starley Basil, seated on his corner stool a bit away from the others continued full time on his composition. Starley was particularly fond of Johnny's pickled sausage.

As the afternoon wore on and three o'clock approached, Johnny warned them that it was time to get their finished versions polished up. There was silence again for a few minutes as they turned back to their pencils and tried to come up with something that was worthy of a quart of beer and a pickled sausage. Most of them didn't make it.

"OK, It's time to turn in your masterpieces," Johnny said and he moved along the bar to pick them up. "Be sure you sign them." They all began folding their papers and handing them in except for Glenn Tink, who was lost in thought. He didn't even realize Johnny was standing in front of him asking for his paper.

"C'mon, Glenn, you so proud of it you don't want to part with it?" Johnny asked. "Let's have it."

"Oh, oh, yeah," said Glenn, suddenly realizing that everyone was waiting for him. "Just skip mine, Johnny, I'm no good at this shit."

"Never mind that," Johnny said, and he pulled the paper from under Glenn's hand. "Everybody's in this contest except me and I'm the judge. And I don't want to hear any pissin' and moanin' from the losers. This judging is going to be subjective." "What the hell does that mean?" Donkey Nuts asked.

"It means it ain't goin' to be fair," Willard told him. "Here, here, I won't have anyone casting doubt on the integrity of my selection," said Johnny.

"I didn't. I just said it wouldn't be fair," Willard replied. Johnny stacked the papers and shuffled through them until he found Ryhmin' Roy's. "I'm going to start right out with Roy's because he's the one you're all going to be measured against. Here's Roy's poem," and he read slowly:

"I'd give up my last dollar to hear a bluebird holler."

"See, there he goes again," griped Donkey Nuts. "What the hell is that supposed to mean? There ain' a bit of sense to it."

"You're supposed to read your own meaning into it," said Johnny. "You know, from your own way of looking at things."

"Yeah, but a bluebird hollerin'? Who ever heard of a bluebird hollerin'?"

"I don't know, maybe if you got one mad enough," Johnny was beginning to enjoy himself.

"Bull shit, Johnny, There ain't no way in God's world you're goin' to get a holler out of a bluebird," Donkey Nuts said emphatically.

"Well, there you got the whole point of the poem. It just might be damn well worth a dollar to hear one of them cut loose." Johnny was really enjoying himself now and he had to turn his back to the bar so the Donk wouldn't see the grin.

"By God, it would be worth a buck to me to hear one of them little things beller out somethin'," said By God Harry. He had been thinking about Roy's poem and couldn't for the life of him see how that tiny little bird could ever do anything but make the little chirp that it does make. It would be worth at least a buck. "But that's the whole thing, By God," said Donkey Nuts, whose exasperation had him almost shouting. "That god-damned dumb little bird ain't never been able to holler, ain't never goin' to be able to holler, I don't care what you do to piss him off. You can stick a gun in his ear and he still ain't goin' to be able to do nothin' but squeak."

"I don't think birds have ears," said Gordie Alley.

"Then shove it up his god-damned ass!" Donkey Nuts shouted. "You still ain't goin' to get nothin' but a twirp. Them things don't have a holler in 'em and that's a fact of nature and there's nothin' you can do about it or I can do about it or Roy can do about it with his god-damned dumb poem."

"Now, wait a minute, Donk, let's not be hurting anybody's feelings here. I'm the one who has to decide how dumb it is," said Johnny. "Let's get on to the next one. Matter of fact, let's make it yours."

Donkey Nuts was fuming, but his anger gave way to embarrassment as he realized his effort was going to be read in front of everyone. "Can't be any dumber than a blue bird hollerin'," he muttered.

"Roses are red, violets are blue, I'd like to bang Willard's wife, too," Johnny read.

"What!" screamed Willard. "What did he say! Read that again! No, don't read that again! What the hell's going on here!"

"It was just a joke," said a sullen Donkey Nuts, realizing maybe he had been a bit insensitive.

"A joke!" Willard was beside himself. "You say that about my wife in front of everybody and you call it a joke. What the hell."

"I told you it was just a joke. It don't mean nothin'," said Donkey Nuts.

"Oh yeah? Well, what about that 'too' stuff? You trying to say there been other guys around there?"

"No, dammit. I'm not sayin' nothin'. I don't know nothin' and I'm not sayin' nothin'. Just settle down."

"You know something, you must know something or you wouldn't have said it. I knew it, I knew this traveling job was a bad move. I'm all over the county selling cigarettes and every Tom, Dick and Harry is traipsin' in my back door."

"Nobody said that, Willard," said Donkey Nuts, trying to calm the man down. "I don't know what the hell your wife has been doin'. It was supposed to be a funny poem. I didn't mean to get you all riled up."

"Aw, it's not your fault, Donk. I been suspecting something for some time. Coming home and finding her all slicked up washing the dishes. Who gets all fancied up to wash dishes? And where are dirty dishes coming from in my house? I don't eat no breakfast and I don't get home until night. Damn, I knew this job was a bad move."

No one pointed out to Willard that he had been traveling the county selling cigarettes for 23 years. In fact, no one knew what to do. It was an awkward few minutes sitting in front of a man who had just told a collective audience that he thought his wife was playing around on him. Donkey Nuts cursed himself for writing the poem. He didn't know Willard's wife and had no desire to. He didn't know what she looked like, but he figured if she was married to Willard, she couldn't be much.

Johnny put the whole thing to rest as best he could by giving Willard something he could at least dwell on for awhile. "Look at it this way, Willard, Chances are she isn't fooling around and is getting dressed up just for you. You know, trying to get some of the old romance going again. Then again, if she is fooling around, at least it's got her fixing herself up real nice before you get home. There aren't too many husbands who can say their wives are all prettied up when they get home."

"That's for sure. My old lady looks like she's been out wrestling hogs by the time I get home," said Glenn Tink.

"I know what you mean," agreed Donkey Nuts, eager to help take a little of the hurt off Willard. "My wife don't put on a decent looking dress except for church on Sunday and then she has that changed quick as she gets home. Doesn't even give me time to get next to her before she's into her old clothes again." The others at the bar agreed that it would be a rare sight to come home and find their wives in anything but their old housedresses.

"So you see what I mean, Willard?" said Johnny. "Chances are she's doing it for you. And if she's not, you still ought to be able to do yourself some good because she's not going to want to get you suspicious."

Willard was doing his best to follow the reasoning and it all began to make a certain amount of sense to him. Anything would be better than what he had been getting. His romancing had about petered out over the last few years and he had more than once remarked that it was a little like living with your sister. Maybe she was trying to change all that. And if not, well, it was like Johnny said, she wasn't in any position to say no. Willard began to feel better. As a matter of fact, he could hardly wait for the contest to get over so he could head for home.

Johnny was back to the poems and he selected By God Harry's composition next.

"Wee Willie Winky, my son John, went to bed with his stockings on."

"Now, wait a minute," said Gordie Alley. "That sounds awful familiar. I think I heard that before."

"Yeah, me too," said Donkey Nuts. "That ain't no original." "That's right, Harry," Johnny said, turning to the big man. "That's an old children's poem. Been around for years. You can't use that. You don't want to be guilty of plagarism do you?"

"By God, no," said Harry, wondering what the hell Johnny was talking about. All he knew is that he had wracked his brain and the only poetry he could remember was back when he was real small and his mother would recite things to him in a sing song voice at the kitchen table. The words hadn't meant much to him, but he had enjoyed the smooth, pretty way she had said them. It was one of the few pleasant memories Harry had of an otherwise harsh and rugged childhood. It didn't seem fair to him that one of the few happy things he could remember didn't count, but he wasn't about to argue with Johnny who he counted as one of the few good people he had ever met. And it did bother him that he wouldn't have a shot at the quart of beer and pickled sausage.

Johnny went on to read a couple of more selections that were rather mundane and then he picked up another one.

"All I got here is a blank piece of paper," he said. "Whose is it?"

No one answered so he laid it down. He picked up the last one and a broad grin spread across his face. He began to chuckle and then he began to laugh. He looked at it for a few more seconds, set it down and went over and got the quart of beer out of the cooler and a pickled sausage out of the jar. "The contest is over, gents," he said and took the beer and the sausage down to the corner of the bar and set them down in front of a delighted Starley Basil.

Donkey Nuts picked up Starley's winning entry and they all looked at it. In labored printed letters it read:

"Pis on it."

There was no argument, no hard feelings. They all congratulated Starley who just grinned his empty-mouth grin and toasted himself right from the bottle.

"Glenn, that must have been your blank piece of paper. How come you didn't at least write something down?" Johnny asked. But Glenn didn't answer. "What the hell's the matter with you?" Johnny asked. "You've been out of it all afternoon."

Glenn only half heard what Johnny was saying. He turned to Rhymin' Roy who was sitting next to him.

"Tell me again, Roy. You sure it was a REAL redhead and a REAL blonde?"

THE CRUEL FACTS OF LIFE

"HE'S GOT TO BE just about the toughest son of a bitch that ever walked and the meanest," Willard Klemp insisted. "The guy is just plain rotten." He was talking about Hans Schmidt, the Teutonic wrestler he had seen cripple a guy the night before on television.

"That skinhead ain't so much," snorted Emery Linfoot. "It's just that he's so dirty. I don't know how the refs let him get away with it. Vern Gagne would get his sleeper hold on him and send that Kraut off to lullaby land."

"I don't know if Gagne could take him or not, but Argentina Rocca would have tied him up in no time, I bet," said Clancy Rierdon.

Like the rest of the country in the mid-1950s, they were caught up in the mania that was professional wrestling. Everyone talked about wrestling and how brutal it was and how blind the referees were. Each of Johnny's customers had a favorite wrestler, but more important, they each had a wrestler they hated with a passion.

Johnny refused to put a television set in The Club because he felt it would stifle the conversation he enjoyed so much. He would bring a set in for the World Series but that was all. So Club members would watch wrestling at home or somewhere else and then come into Johnny's the next day to talk about it. Professional wrestling was the only so-called sport where there were more contestants being cheered against than for. A unique and healthy hatred developed for some of the bad guys like Hans Schmidt who played with a defenseless opponent like a cat with a mouse. At least Johnny considered it healthy. Here right in front of them were living examples of how not to be. No kid was going to want to grow up to be like Hans Schmidt. He was an object lesson in bad.

The night before Hans Schmidt had crippled a baby-faced blonde Adonis named Johnny Straight with a series of illegal death-threatening blows to the back of the head and The Club membership was outraged.

"I'm telling you, I wouldn't wait a minute to see what kind of pattern I could lay on that bastard with some Number 4 shot," said Willard. "He just kept beating on the poor kid and the referee didn't do nothin'. I can't believe he couldn't see what was going on."

"I don't think they dare to do anything," said Sammy Griney. "I've seen when those refs have got knocked right on their ass. Even knocked right out cold. Them wrestlers try to make it look like an accident, but you can tell they're doing it on purpose. They're just trying to get the refs out of the way so they can pull some shit."

"Well, if they can't handle it, they shouldn't be in there," said Emery. "Somebody's got to make these guys stick to the rules. They're going to kill somebody one of these days and ruin the sport. It's the guys that can't wrestle very good that do the dirty stuff. You don't see Gagne doing none of that and he was an Olympic wrestler."

Emery was a true believer when it came to wrestling. He was a 30-year-old solidly built tow-head with a round red face who came down off the farm to hire out as a carpenter. He wasn't so much slow-witted as he was naive. He and his brothers had spent most of their lives helping their father squeeze what they could out of the rock pile they worked as a dairy farm.

There was little time for reading and no money for a TV. Some Hank Williams and Little Jimmy Dickens on the radio was about his only cultural exposure. He had tried out for sports in school but, despite his strength, was too slow and awkward to accomplish much. Emery was well-liked by everyone because he was a thoroughly decent man. He had a farm boy's shyness that made him a natural for ribbing by guys in The Club. But he knew the ribbing was good-natured and he actually enjoyed the attention. Shy as he was, he still felt more comfortable in The Club than any other place in town.

Emery had taken a small apartment up over Andrews hardware store and his first paycheck went for a TV. It only had a nine-inch screen, but his apartment was so small he had to sit up close to it anyway so it didn't really matter.

Emery became a wrestling nut. He never went out on wrestling night, but made popcorn and Koolaid and fiddled with the set until he got the best picture he could and spent the night raging against the villains and cheering for the heroes. He was too quiet a guy to make a big show about it, but inside he would be all wound up and wishing he could get his hands on the Hans Schmidts and the Killer Kowalskis of this world. There was a right and a wrong here that was easy for him to understand. He would get furious with the referees when they would look the other way while a particularly rotten character rubbed soap in the eyes of a God-fearing, clean-living yes ma'am opponent.

He would occasionally get so riled that he would jump to his feet and plead with the ref to turn around, turn around and see what injustices were being done behind his back. One night he was so angry he forgot he had the pitcher of Koolaid in his hand and sprayed it all over the room as he waved frantically to the referee to pay attention, turn around and keep Mr. USA from being strangled by a ring rope.

Emery bought wrestling hook, line and sinker. TV and wrestling were both fairly new to the town and, although most of The Club members professed not to believe it, they still weren't entirely sure and many of them secretly cheered on their heroes and developed deep-seated hatred for their favorite villains. It didn't seem like anyone could take that much punishment, but these were mighty big guys and they were in awfully good shape. Still, it didn't seem likely that you could just about rip a guy's arm right out of the socket and a minute later have him lift you over his head with it. It had most in The Club wavering, but not Emery. For him, these were super athletes a cut above the rest of the sports world. They could take the pain and punishment because they had more guts than other athletes. These gladiators believed in laying it all on the line.

"Did you see Yukon Eric last night? Rocca came off the ring ropes and got him with both knees right in the belly. It's a wonder it didn't bust his gut wide open." Glenn Tink and Willard Klemp were discussing the previous night's main event.

"You ain't never going to hurt Yukon Eric in the belly," interrupted Emery who had been listening in.

"Oh, yeah, why not?" Tink asked.

"Because he's got the strongest stomach in the world," Emery said. "I read where he trains by letting them shoot cannon balls at his stomach."

"Good God, Emery, get serious,' said Willard impatiently. "There ain't no way in hell you can take a cannon ball in the gut and not come out without one hell of a big dimple. It would tear a hole right through to Tuesday."

"No, it's true," Emery persisted. "I read he has one of those circus cannons and they load it up and blast away. They probably don't use as much powder, but I read that it's true."

"You'd believe anything," Willard said. "As far as I'm concerned, it's bullshit. It doesn't make sense to begin with. Besides, I got my doubts about old Eric. With all the hair he's got down over his ears, he looks like a fruit."

"Didn't you know about that?" said Emery. "He grew his hair long because Killer Kowalski bit one of his ears off. I thought everybody knew about that."

"Yeah, Willard, I heard that, too," said Tink. "He's supposed to have chomped right through Yukon's left ear. I heard he went over to the edge of the ring and spit it at the audience. People were getting sick and everything."

"Now, that's got to be bullshit," said Willard. "You could have him arrested for something like that."

"Yukon didn't want him arrested. I read where he said he just wanted to get Kowalski back in the ring," said Emery. "They've got a big grudge match coming up next month and you know where it's going to be? Right down in Binghamton."

"Boy, I'd give my left nut to see that match," said Tink. "It's gotta be a blood bath."

"Why don't you all go?" asked Johnny. "It's only a half hour away and you've got a month to save up the money. Glen works right down there. He could pick up the tickets on his way home. Sounds like a big night to me."

That got them all started. They kicked it around for awhile and decided it was going to be too exciting a night to miss. Each assessed his own precarious financial situation and decided it would be worth it to sacrifice some other worldly pleasures for what promised to be a night of get-even mayhem. Emery was the most excited of all. He had seldom been to Binghamton and when he did go it was in the pickup to get something that couldn't be bought in Mill Town. He had never gone for anything as exciting as a wrestling match. They all agreed to get their money to Tink by the end of the week so he would be sure to get good seats. The Kalurah Temple wasn't all that big and the tickets were bound to go fast.

The following Monday Tink walked in with tickets for himself, Willard, Emery, Donkey Nuts and Clancy Rierdon, who surprised everybody by deciding to join them for a night out. The tickets were good ones. Fourth row center. Now all they had to do was wait.

Waiting wasn't easy. For the next three weeks, conversation at The Club almost always got around to the upcoming Yukon Eric-Killer Kowalski match. Who would win? How would he win? Who would take the worst beating? How was Eric going to avenge losing an ear? It would have to be something pretty gruesome to make up for the loss of an ear.

"Maybe he'll pop out one of Kowaksi's eyes," said Tink, wincing at the thought.

"Good God, Glenn, he wouldn't go that far," said Willard, "They've got to have some limits on what they can do."

"I don't know, those refs never seem to catch the real dirty stuff," Emery said. "They can get away with about anything they want to. I've heard of eye-gouging before." It began to occur to Emery that his stomach was not up to witnessing Kowalksi's eye popping out of his face and squirting into the audience.

"Naw, I don't think they'd let that happen," said Donkey Nuts. "He'll probably do something like stomp on his throat and crush his Adams apple. They say that's about as painful as anything that can happen to you."

"Well, it's going to have to be something pretty bad to make up for an ear ..." and the conversation continued.

The day of the big match finally arrived, and they all gathered at The Club in mid-afternoon. Most of them had quit work early to get ready and Willard had doubled up on his cigarette route the day before to allow him some extra time. They were all going in Tink's car and agreed to meet at The Club at 3 o'clock. They figured on a few beers there and some dinner at the Pig Stand on the way into Binghamton. Emery had brought a copy of Wrestling News that he hoped to get Yukon Eric to sign if he got the chance.

"You better hope he's going to be in shape to sign it," Donkey Nuts said. "That cannibal might do a job on his other ear if he gets the chance."

"He ain't going to get the chance. Yukon will destroy him. The killer is going to get killed. He'll be lucky if he ever wrestles again," said Emery.

"Well, I wouldn't bet on it. That Kowalski is tougher than horse manure and meaner than Peg Cavanaugh. He's not going to just stand there and let your man do a dance on him," Donkey Nuts said.

"Don't worry. I read that Yukon got suckered the last time. Kowalski got him in the back of the head with a chair. He snuck up on him."

"How the hell is he going to sneak up on him when they're out there in the middle of everything?"

"I don't know how he did it, but he did and the ref didn't do anything even after he bit his ear off. I read that Yukon was bleeding so much they had to stop the fight."

"Well, you better hope he doesn't sneak up on him again or he won't have anything left to hear with," said Donkey Nuts.

As they talked, Willard glanced out the front window. "Would you look at that boat that just pulled up. What a battlewagon!" They all looked out just as a gleaming white 1956 Cadillac convertible pulled up out front. There were no white Cadillacs in Mill Town or anywhere near Mill Town. Not new ones. There might be one or two beat up, rusted out 1948 or 1949 models in Sid's Junk Yard on the edge of town, but nothing that looked like the brand new limousine they were staring at out front.

It was a warm afternoon and the top was down. The two guys in it looked over the front of The Club and talked together briefly. They both got out of the car.

"Jesus, look at the size of those guys," said Tink as the two men stood up and looked around. They were huge. The driver was wearing a powder blue leisure suit that cost more than Tink made in a month and the suit covered a white silk shirt open at the man's bull neck. He had black hair cut close to his head and in front of it was a beat up countenance that looked like it had been carved out of rock. A nose that had been flattened and widened countless times. A knotted forehead that combined with high protruding cheekbones to form hedge rows for eyes that set deep in his head. He had a wide, ragged mouth and a broad jutting chin. He was at least six and a half feet tall and fronted a barrel chest that tapered to a 34-inch waist. His enormous fingers carried walnut-sized rings on the fourth and fifth digits of each hand.

His passenger was no less impressive and was even bigger. He was wearing a salmon cashmere coat sweater and soft white slacks. A mint green turtleneck shirt rose out of the sweater to encircle a 20-inch neck. He had a massive round face that seemed to absorb his features. His eyes, nose and mouth looked as if they belonged to a much smaller face. His features were also upstaged by a mane of blond hair that flowed down over the top of the turtleneck. It also curled down over both ears like a helmet. He was a couple of inches taller than the driver and 20 pounds heavier. The cashmere sweater bulged from the enormous muscles straining at it as he moved to the door of The Club.

"Look at those dudes, They're dressed prettier than women," said Donkey Nuts as they all stared out the window.

"You better not let them hear you, Donk, I don't think even you can handle them," Clancy warned.

"They're comin' in. I wonder what the hell they want in here," Tink said as they hurried back over to the bar. They took up their positions and tried to act as nonchalant as they could while waiting for two of the flashiest things ever to hit this town to make their appearance.

The two giants stepped into the bar and looked around. They checked out the huddle of customers at the end of the bar pretending not to notice them and then settled for one of Johnny's little two-chair tables in the front corner of the room away from the bar. They sat down and the table disappeared. They looked as if they were sitting at furniture in kindergarten.

"Hey, buddy, how bout a couple of beers and a menu?" the black-haired one called to Johnny in a rumbling voice.

"You got it," said Johnny, and he grabbed a couple of bottles of Stegmaiers and a pair of wrinkled, faded menus and took them to the table.

"What's this town?" Black Hair asked.

"This is Mill Town, Pa.," Johnny said.

"Oh, yeah? How far is it to Binghamton?"

"It's only about 25 miles. You go straight through town and keep on Route 11 right in to Binghamton," Johnny said.

"That ain't too bad, that gives us plenty of time," said Yellow Hair. They studied Johnny's skimpy menu briefly and ordered two hamburgers apiece and another beer.

All the time Johnny was waiting on them, the men at the bar kept trying to toss casual glances their way. Emery, who had been watching the closest, slid to the corner of the bar and began leafing through a stack of magazines.

Willard watched the two men in quiet conversation and was dying to know what they were talking about. He decided he should check the cigarette machine that was just behind them in the corner. He took his keys out and walked over and opened the machine and began counting the cartons.

"God, I hate havin' to stop in these dumps," Black Hair was saying as he slugged down his second beer right from the bottle. "This place ain't even on the map."

"You don't see me dancin' for joy, do ya?" said Yellow Hair. "But what else we goin' to do. Have you figured out where that motel is yet?"

"Yeah, it's supposed to be right on this road right outside of Binghamton. Left hand side with a big sign. Herb says it's close enough a cab won't cost you only a couple of bucks to get into town."

"Well, the next time I'm drivin' and you're taking the cab. And I'm goin' to tell Herb he has to come up with better arrangements than this shit. I want to eat in a decent restaurant, not some crud hole in the middle of nowhere."

"What the hell else we going to do? Once we split up, you can eat anyplace you want. It didn't make sense for both of us to drive all the way up from Reading. Once we get out of this place tonight, maybe we can find a decent spot before we get to Buffalo. Who you got in Buffalo?"

"I don't know. Herb didn't tell me. Might be a fill-in."

"Well, it ain't forever and you can't beat the money. I sure as hell don't know any better way to get poontang either." "That's another thing. Herb only got us one room, the cheap bastard. What if I do some good for myself. I don't wan't you sittin' there watchin' me."

Black Hair laughed a growling laugh. "Watch you? Why the hell would I want to watch you? I ain't goin' to learn nothin' from you. I saw what you can do in Reading. I wouldn't touch that with a stick."

"She wasn't all that bad. Beats that fat cow you were rolling on, or rollin' off is more like it."

"Hey, I like 'em big. Gives you somethin' to hold on to." Willard closed the cigarette machine and headed back to the bar. He urgently moved everyone to the corner of the bar. "You won't God-damned believe this, but I think I know something."

Emery, who had been staring in shock at the magazine, said, "I know it, too. I don't believe it." Right there in front of him on page 19 of the Wrestling

News were the two monsters who had just dropped a $5 tip on the table and were heading out the door. "Those bastards. Those dirty bastards," said Tink. "Bit his ear off, did he? Bit it off my ass. He probably kissed it off." Emery just sat staring at the magazine as the others talked of betrayal and deception and how you just couldn't trust anyone anymore. He looked up to see the others preparing to leave and tossed the magazine on the bar and followed them. Starley Basil grinned and nodded as Emery passed him going out the door.

Johnny greeted Starley as he came in. "Starley, you do a good job today and I've got a real bonus for you. Five fourth row center seats at the Temple. You can't beat them."

SOMETIMES IT'S SURVIVAL OF THE FOULEST

"I TRADED MY HEN and I got me a mare and then I rode from fair to fair."

Clevis Randle was in fine voice. He stretched every note and drawled every word to get everything he could out of them. He had a way of starting each line of a song by swinging his face up over his right shoulder and bringing it down in a swooping motion just as he hit the first couple of words. By the time he had completed his swoop he was three or four words into the song and was straight on with his audience, which in this particular case was a moderately plastered Henry Wabash.

Henry liked to travel with Clevis because of the attention they received. There was no one in Susquehanna County who was better liked or more fun than Clevis Randle. He generated a good feeling everywhere he went. Clevis was like a pot-bellied stove on a cold day. People gathered around him for the warmth. He was never known to be down, never known to be moody, never known to be mean. He was ready for fun at the drop of a note.

"Come a wing, come a wobble, come a Jack, come a straddle, come a John go daddy, come a long way home," Clevis warbled at the conclusion of one of his favorites as Henry closed his eyes and savored the last refrain along with his shot and a beer.

By the time Clevis had finished the first song, a half dozen people had gathered around ready for the next one. Clevis' voice was not about to win the Arthur Godfrey Talent Scout contest. It was a nasal, gravelly voice the likes of which could be heard any night of the week on Wheeling, West Virginia radio. He had a good ear and always stayed on key even after he had dipped a bit too deep into the well. But the magnetic feature of Clevis' singing was the fun. He had fun in his voice and when he let it out, it spread all over the place.

Clevis had a small farm and a few head of dairy cattle which he was up at 4:30 in the morning to take care of before he drove into work at the only real industry in town, a factory that made freezers and pop coolers. He was the hardest worker in the place and also one of the hardest drinkers. He was farm-raised and strong and had the red cheeks common to men who spent most of their time outdoors and also common to the men who had put down too many whiskeys. Clevis had done that. He often said he drank just to keep his wife happy. He said she lived to worry and she did her best worrying when he was drinking. "Old Blanche is going to be happier than hell tonight," he would say after a particularly long session in The Club. "I just got to get home and watch her enjoy herself." And then that face would open into a wide grin beginning at the corners of his eyes and working its way down.

Clevis was right. Blanche worried about everything. It was her nature to fret and stew and if everything was going along fine and dandy, she would worry about when it was going to turn around and go the other way. Clevis accepted her outlook on life and would occasionally reassure her. "Now, Ma, everything's going to be all right," he would say and go on about his business.

On this particular day his business was to enjoy himself as much as he could. It had been an especially hot July afternoon when he got out of work and his son was home on leave from the Army and had offered to do evening chores for him. Clevis had stopped at the American store to get the Spic and Span that Blanche wanted and he ran into Henry Wabash coming out of Adams hardware store with a roll of wire mesh.

"Hey, Henry, how the hell are ya?" asked Clevis.

"Guess I'm alright considering I'm about to dry right up and blow away."

"You've got a point there. You surely have. It's a mite warm, that's for sure."

"A mite warm? It was 93 degrees over at the drug store and that thermometer ain't even in the sun."

"Well, it's bound to cool sooner or later, but right now the best thing to do is get in out of it. It's got my throat drier than a popcorn fart. Think we ought to do something about that?"

"I don't know, Clevis, I'm supposed to fix the rabbit cage. Goddamned dogs got another one last night. My wife's madder than hell about it 'cause I told her I would fix it last week."

"She doesn't expect you to work your ass off in this heat does she? We'll just go have a couple and by then it'll cool down some and you can work in comfort."

"OK, A couple it is and then I got to get goin'," and they headed up the street to The Club.

"I went down to tend a meetin' just the other afternoon when I heard them shout and sing."

Clevis was on a roll now with an appreciative audience gathered around himself and Henry. For the most part, Henry was content to let Clevis take it solo and just enjoy the attention Clevis was bringing to them both. But every once in a while he felt inspired to hum along for a bar or two. He would dip his chin and hum his best hum and then sit back contented that he and Clevis were really wowing them today.

"Hey, Clevis, how about doing that one with the hula hula girls shakin' their titties?" Shake Ketter always asked Clevis for the same song.

"Well, now, you think we ought to do that one? I reckon you're probably right. That's probably just what we ought to do," and Clevis began singing, "Everybody does it in Hawai-i-ah."

As the songs wore on and Henry's rabbit cage repairs were forgotten, The Club began to fill up with members sipping relief from the swelter.

Clevis took a break to down a shot and a beer just about the time a ruckus got started at the other end of the bar. It was Ed Hooker and one of the out-of-town guys working on the new highway starting to mix it up. It didn't last long. Ed got his hands up in front of his eyes, blocking out everything including his opponent, who stood there looking puzzled. He waited for a minute, shrugged and pasted Ed right above his left ear. Ed went down liked a poled ox. He lay there on the floor in front of the bar until everyone got tired of tripping over him and a couple of them dragged him outside and left him sitting up against the building.

A while later, Clevis was in the middle of another song when he looked up and saw Ed coming in the back door. He never even made it up to the bar this time. He tried to get around the pool table but bumped into another highway worker and ruined his shot. In a split second, Ed was into his fighting stance and in another split second he had taken a roundhouse left behind his right ear and collapsed like a throw rug over the pool table. To get the game going again, three of them picked Ed up and carried him back out front and set him up against the building again.

Ed was sitting there glassy-eyed with two knots on his head just as Emilia Catterwaite and Eunice Hample arrived for the Mill Town Library Board meeting. It was particularly vexing to the seven members of the library board, all good Christian women, that the only place to park was on the other side of The Club. They had no choice but to use the sidewalk in front of The Club and they did that with great trepidation. Who knew what despicable thing might come out of the front of that place to confront them. Well, they didn't have to worry about it that evening. It was already there in grimy old Ed staring into nowhere and wetting his pants just as Mrs. Catterwaite and Miss Hample walked by.

"Do you believe that? Don't even look, Eunice, disgusting, that's what it is, just disgusting," said Mrs. Catterwaite and the two of them fixed their eyes straight down the sidewalk trying to ignore the soaking pile of wet clothes sprawled up against the building.

"You don't know what one of those people might do if they got the chance. They aren't above doing just about anything," Mrs. Catterwaite said.

Miss Hample, who had never so much as caught a man's eye in all her 62 years, could very well have wondered desperately what just about anything might consist of, but whatever it was she certainly had none of it to fear from Ed Hooker, whose only suggestive act was to scratch his wet crotch as he began to come around.

The two women disappeared into the great stone library just in time to miss seeing Ed roll over on all fours and to miss hearing Clevis roll into an uptempo version of "I drink my coffee from an old tin can..."

Clevis was singing and Hank was humming when Ed managed to stagger through the back door again. This time he didn't even make it to the pool table. Sammy Griney came out of the men's room and threw the door open wide. It whacked Ed, who had been trying to steady his way along one wall to the bar. Ed was ready for the attack. He sort of wheeled around to confront the back-jumper and by the time he was turned around facing the door, he had his fists up in front of his eyes ready for anything. There he stood a foot and a half from the door waiting for his assailant to strike again. It didn't strike for about 10 minutes until By God Harry had to relieve himself of a gallon and a half of Stegmaiers and tried to get into the bathroom. He opened the door and nudged Ed with it. "By God, Ed, get out of the way. I got to piss something fierce," By God Harry said.

But Ed Hooker was not about to let his concentration be broken by chit chat. He stood ready for that door to just try something, ready to counter attack at the slightest provocation. By God Harry had to slide his bulk sideways through the door so as not to cause Ed to spring into action.

Ed didn't spring for another 10 minutes. He stood at the ready staring down that door just waiting for another assault. Ed's strength was counterpunching. Everyone who used the bathroom just opened the door a little bit and slid through without disturbing Ed. They were all being real gentlemen about not bothering him. All except Peg Cavanaugh. She wasn't being a gentleman about it at all.

"Move, Ed, I gotta wee wee," she said. Ed held his stance. "Listen, just because you pissed your pants doesn't mean I'm going to piss mine," she said, "Now move."

Ed held fast.

"Let's go. Hooker, out of the way. I gotta go."

Ed clenched his fists a little tighter.

"You goddamned drunk, I'll move you," and Peg grabbed the door knob and swung the door open, slamming Hooker's fists into his face and sending him flying back against the wall. He folded down the wall like a venetian blind and laid there. He was out of the way so everyone left him alone for a few minutes, but the urine-beer smell drifting up from Ed finally got to some of the pool players and they carefully took hold of him and took him back out front.

By this time, Clevis was getting a little concerned about old Ed. He had known him for years so had more reason than most not to be concerned about him, but that was the way Clevis was. "Maybe we should see to Ed," he said to Hank.

"To hell with him. I wouldn't worry about him," said Hank. "Well, it seems he's had about all the beatin' a man should have for one night. Maybe we should just see that he don't get himself killed."

Hank followed Clevis out front where they found Hooker in a fetal position under Rhymin' Roy William's 1952 Ford pickup. He was taking a comfortable nap, snuggling up to his asphalt pillow. He was building up his reserve strength.

"Now, isn't that a picture. That old fella's sleepin' just like a baby," said Clevis. "I believe he could sleep on a hot stove when he gets too much in him."

"He don't smell like no baby," said Hank as they reached under the truck to drag Hooker out by his shoes. "He smells like my cesspool."

Clevis was forced to agree. Along with the oil and the grease, the dirt he seemed to grow by himself, the beer and the urine, Ed in his nocturnal slumber had messed his pants. The smell all but rolled off him like a heat wave.

"Jesus, he's rank," Hank complained as he sought the upwind side of Hooker. "What you going to do with him, Clevis? You can't put him in your car. Blanche'd never set foot in it again and I don't blame her."

"Well, we can't leave the poor bastard here. Somebody's liable to run over him. Tell you what, you keep an eye on him and I'll go get the car. We can put him in the trunk 'til he comes around. That shouldn't stink things up too much. Besides, I already got a bag of fertilizer in there so it shouldn't make much difference."

Clevis got the car and pulled up next to Ed. He opened the trunk and he and Hank took deep breaths, reached down, got a hold of Hooker and hoisted him into the trunk. They laid him down with his head on the bag of fertilizer and closed the lid. It was only a little after dark and the day's searing temperature hadn't begun to cool down much. Clevis and Hank had worked up a good sweat handling Hooker. Clevis wiped the wet from his eyebrows.

"He'll be OK for now. We can check on him in a little while," he said. "I don't know about you but all that work's got me thirstier than a bullhead. Suppose we ought to do something about that? Don't you think that'd be a good idea?"

"Might's well," Hank replied, "My old lady's goin' to kill me anyhow. Might's well be later than sooner." They returned to The Club and their audience. They sang up every song Clevis knew which took a considerable length of time and an even more considerable number of shots and beers. Hank had fashioned sort of a stove pipe out of the roll of wire mesh and had enlisted Donkey Nuts' help to slip it down over Sammy Griney's head as he stood at the bar. Sammy's arms were pinned at his sides and Donkey Nuts held him while Hank looped several strands of baling wire around the mesh to hold Sammy tight.

Sammy squawked and screeched and swore for a while but it did him no good. The roll of mesh came just about up to his chin which didn't impede his drinking, but having his arms pinned at his sides did. That is what he was most upset about. He continued to whine and bitch until Donkey Nuts took a bottle of beer and stuck it in his mouth. Sammy took a good swig and quieted down. The talk and music continued and Sammy joined in just as if it was the most natural thing in the world to be standing there all wrapped up in a roll of wire mesh. Every couple of minutes Donkey Nuts would feed him a swig or two from the bottle and he would even take a bar rag and wipe his chin when he got too much. He did everything but burp the little guy.

As the night wore on and the songs ran down, Clevis and Hank reached the point of too-late-to-go-home. It was getting harder to stay on key and harder to remember exactly what errands they were on when they ran into each other that afternoon. What mattered at the moment was that they were having a great time. Everything else could wait until tomorrow.

But the fatal flaw that afflicts just about every barroom in the world finally caught up with The Club – time for last call.

Club members began to peel off and reluctantly leave, knowing that where they were going wasn't going to be half as much fun and that in another several hours they would awake to face another damn day of work.

Hank had unwound Sammy and got his wire mesh back and he and Clevis stood out front taking turns drawing on one of the four quarts of Stegmaiers they had bought for travelers. "Hell, Clevis, there ain't no sense in my goin' home now. Bess'd just start givin' me shit and one thing I don't need right now is shit."

"Well, why don't you come on home with me? You can sleep on the porch and I can give you a ride back in when I take Blanche shopping."

Hank agreed that was probably the best course for him at the moment and he and Clevis climbed into the car and headed for Clevis' place two miles out of town. Clevis pulled up the long driveway and parked alongside the old farmhouse. It needed painting and a few other repairs that Clevis was planning to get around to one of these days.

Clevis took the Spic and Span in one hand and a quart of Stegmaiers in the other and headed for the house. Hank took a quart of Stegmaiers in each hand and followed him.

"Is that you, Clevis?" the voice came out of the darkness as they stepped on to the enclosed porch.

"Yeah, it's me, Ma. What are you doin' up this late?"

"How'd you expect me to sleep with not knowin' where you were or anything. How did I know what might have happened to you? You could have run off the road or somethin'. How did I know you didn't get hurt at work or somethin'? Anything could have happened."

"Well, it didn't. The only thing that happened is that I ran into Hank here and we stopped for a couple and got to singin' and Hank decided he'd stay the night."

"Oh, is that you, Hank?" Blanche peered into the dark porch. "How's your wife? You know I keep tellin' him I get worried sick when he don't come home because who knows what could happen when he's out like that with the drinkin' and all. How's your boy Billy? I bet he's as big as you are. It's no wonder I'm getting gray sittin' around wonderin' where he's at when he don't come home like he's supposed to. What am I supposed to think? You have a daughter, too, don't you, Hank?"

"Yes, ma'am. They're all fine," Hank said, hoping the conversation wouldn't go much further and he could get down to working on one of those quarts of Stegmaiers.

"You just go on back to bed, Ma. Hank and I are going to sit up for a few minutes and then I'll be to bed. I'll fix Hank up a place here on the porch. We ain't goin' to be too long."

"Well, I hope not, 'cause you know I can't sleep good when you're up and wanderin' around. And the way my back has been achin' me, I got to have all the rest I can get. Douglas said he'd do the chores again in the morning so you might as well sleep in for awhile. You got to get some sleep once in awhile."

"Don't worry, Ma, I'll get some sleep. Now just try to rest," and Clevis steered Blanche back into the house. He came back and sat down in the big wicker chair that he enjoyed leaning back in and watching the sunsets out over the barn. Hank sat on the porch glider that was to be his bed for the night and reached for the Stegmaiers Clevis had set down on the porch floor.

"It sure is nice out here in the country," said Hank. "It couldn't get much quieter." He was feeling the beer and the shots and the heat and the combination was draining the last of the energy out of him the way he was draining the last of the beer out of the bottle. He set the bottle down and was trying to think of what else he wanted to say when he slowly folded over on his side on the glider and was asleep before Clevis could even offer him a pillow.

Clevis took the other two quarts of beer into the refrigerator. He thought for a moment about opening another but then figured Blanche would worry just that much longer so he closed the refrigerator door and went to bed.

Blanche was true to her word and didn't wake Clevis until it was mid-morning. Clevis ordinarily beat the sun up, but on mornings after a good sing-along it was a whole lot harder to drag out and get going. Blanche always had to get him up on those mornings.

Hank was a different story. On the best day of his life, his wife had to cajole, bully and just about kick him out of bed to get him started. She had to about stand there and watch him get dressed or he would be back in the sack in a second. This day was no different.

Clevis walked out on the porch and found Hank in exactly the position he had left him. He talked to him and shook him a few times until Hank finally blinked and looked around, not knowing where he was. Things finally began to sink in and he sat up, suddenly desperate to remember where to find the bathroom. Clevis anticipated his need. "Just step out behind the barn, podner. Blanche is in the bathroom and she'll probably be there most the morning."

Hank hurried off the porch and ran smack into the sunshine. The glare and the heat staggered him about as much as the beer had. By the time he had made it to the barn and back he was feeling faint and sat down at the kitchen table with Clevis. "My God, Clevis, that heat is somethin'. It must be a hundred or so. It's enough to take the strength right out of you." "She's a scorcher all right. Not the kind of day to be shovelin' shit. More the kind of day to be countin' eggs, don't you think?"

"I'll tell ya, I've felt better than I do right now, heat or no heat. I could use a little somethin' to bring me back a bit."

"Well, we've got two quarts of Dr. Clevis' guaranteed pick-me-up tonic right in the refrigerator. Blanche ain't goin' to like it much, but I guess you could call this a medical emergency." "You damn well could. A genuine emergency is what it is. This here patient is critical."

Clevis got the two quarts of beer and gave one to Hank. Each man opened his own and took a swig.

"I'm goin' to get killed when I get home and there's no sense gettin' it on an empty stomach," Hank said as he took another pull on the bottle. "I don't care if Bess does get all over me. I had a fine time last night, Clevis. I sure do like that singin'."

"Yep, it was an enjoyable evening. It's just too bad it has to take so much out of you the next day. But I guess that's the only way to keep us honest, don't you think? If we woke up feelin' great, we'd be right back at it and then where would we be?" Clevis said, taking a pull on his bottle. "At least we've got to be feelin' a whole lot better than old Ed ..." Clevis stopped suddenly and looked at Hank. It hit Hank at the same time.

"Good God, he must be cooked!" Clevis jumped up from the table and ran through the door off the porch and out to the car. Hank hurried along behind him. It was so hot the trunk handle smarted Clevis' fingers. He opened the trunk and reeled back, his knees buckling. The stench that had been bottled up in there fairly flew out of the car. Hank's nervous stomach wouldn't even let him get close.

Clevis took a deep breath and peered into the trunk. There lay Ed in all his reeking glory. He had somehow ripped the bag of fertilizer and his face was now about two-thirds buried in it. He was not moving a muscle and looked like he never would again.

"Hank, I swear he's dead," said Clevis.

"Oh, My God, what are we going to do? What are we going to do with a dead Ed?" Hank still couldn't get himself up close to the car.

Clevis tried for a closer look. Ed's body was all twisted around. Somehow, maybe in the bouncing he'd taken on the way to Clevis' house, his left leg had gotten flung up over his back and had hung up in the spare tire. Both arms were pinned under him as if he were trying to open his fly. His face was glowing red and the one eye that wasn't buried in the fertilizer was half open, staring sightless at a can of Atlantic 40-weight oil.

"I don't know, Hank. The only kin he's got is a brother and he's still in jail as far as I know. He had a wife at one time, but she wised up and took off a long time ago. I don't know anybody who'd claim him."

"Well, he sure as hell can't spend the rest of his days in your trunk. You can't drive around all the time with a corpse."

"You're right there. Maybe we ought to just leave him in there and drive right down to the funeral home now. They ought to know what to do with him."

"You do that, Clevis, and you know who's going to get stuck paying for the funeral? The guy who delivered him, that's who." "Well, I don't mind helpin' him out, but I'm damned if I'm payin' to bury him. He owes me money as it is."

"That's what I'm sayin.' He's goin' to owe you even more money if you take him down there. What's wrong with findin' a spot for him down by the creek? We could fix him up a nice place and then go in town and tell them what happened. Nobody's goin' to care. They'll be glad you found a spot for him."

"I don't know. I'm not sure you're allowed to do that. I think they at least have to take a look at him or something. You know, to show it was natural causes."

"There ain't no one in the world expected Ed Hooker to die of natural causes."

"Well, maybe not, but it seems like we ought to take him into town and show him around a little bit and then come back and bury him. That way we got witnesses."

"You do what you want to, Clevis, but sure as hell you get anywhere near that funeral home and old Ron Yesser's going to be out there claimin' the body and the next thing you know he's goin' to demand that you pay for it."

They stood there in the heat discussing what to do with Ed's remains when the subject of their concern let out a fart that darn near shook the car.

"Jesus to Jesus, Clevis, that corpse just farted! Can they do that? My God, that's scary."

"I don't know if most of them can, but old Ed could cut the cheese if he was sunk in 10 feet of concrete and you would know it, too. But I got a feelin' we've been plannin' Ed's funeral too early." Clevis could see twitching in Ed's steaming face as he made feeble unconscious efforts to rid his mouth of about a half a pound of multipurpose fertilizer.

"Go get one of those beers, Hank, I think he might be startin' to come around."

Hank hurried off for the beer while Clevis got Ed by a shoulder and dragged him half out of the car. Ed was still as limp as a pile of smelly laundry, but there were stronger signs of breathing now that his face was out of the fertilizer. Clevis got him flopped over so he was sprawled face up with his head lying back against a fender. One eye was closed and the other was half open, but it wasn't seeing anything. Hank returned with a quart of beer. Clevis took it and poured a few drops on Ed's parched lips. The beer just rolled down his cheek.

"Maybe he is a goner after all," Clevis said. Ed had never let a drop of beer get by his lips. Clevis tried a few more drops and Ed's instincts began to take over. His lips moved, then they opened a bit and his tongue came out to catch a drop that was threatening to roll off on the ground. Clevis stuck the bottle in his mouth and poured. At first it was like pouring water down a balky drain. The beer would fill Ed's mouth almost to overflowing and Clevis would have to wait until it slowly ran down into his belly.

"By God, I think he's got a plugged up trap," said Clevis as he slowly poured another mouthful. He about used up the quart and Ed was still not showing any signs of functioning on his own so he told Hank to get the other quart.

"What do you mean, Clevis? That's the only quart we got left. You're not going to waste it on him, are you?"

"Hank, the man's about dead. We've got to at least try to get him going again."

"Why don't you just give him some water? That's what you ought to be givin' him."

"Water? Water's just about as foreign to Ed as soap. It'd probably just make him sick. Get that other quart now before we lose him all together."

Hank reluctantly brought the quart and Clevis began to pour it into Ed. This time he began to show some life. The quart wasn't half gone before his other eye opened and both of them began to focus on Clyde.

"Well, hello, Clevis, what are you doin' here?" Ed remarked through cracked lips. He tried to sit up but it was too much of an effort so he laid back down on the fertilizer, trying to figure out why he was staring at the inside of a car trunk.

"Hank and me gave you a ride home last night, Ed. We figured you'd about gotten tired beatin' up on everybody at The Club and could use a rest."

"That right? Did I do pretty good?" Ed asked, dragging himself out of the trunk.

"You was three for three. You had a perfect night."

"Is that a damn fact? It don't surprise me none, though. I figured I was about due. You mind if I use your creek, Clevis? I think I need to wash up."

THE BEST LAID PLANS OF HORNY MEN

"DON'T LOOK NOW, BOYS, but here comes Georgette."

All eyes swung to the front door as Georgette Masters got out of her car and approached The Club. She was a striking woman of 35 who was only moderately attractive but who knew how to arrange herself so that she got the most out of her assets. She was a sharp dresser, chose her colors carefully and bought only quality apparel. She had dark brown hair that always looked as though it had just returned from the beauty parlor. It framed her neatly made up face and a pair of the latest style glasses. Georgette was one woman who looked better with glasses than without. They added a stylish element to rather plain features.

"I wonder who's going to get lucky tonight?" mused Johnny as he watched Georgette's incredible legs carry her through the front door. What Georgette lacked in her face she more than made up for in her body. She was a walking series of curves, full breasted, narrow waist, full hips and as Gordie Alley put it, legs all the way up to her shoulders. By God Harry Hollis referred to her as a healthy heifer and Donkey Nuts Crowley observed that she grew up just about right.

On this particular cool, fall evening, Georgette was wearing one of those clinging knit dresses that accentuated every move of her body. She could not have looked sexier if she had been standing there in the all together which is what every male in The Club was imagining anyway.

"Hi, Johnny, Hi, everybody," Georgette called brightly as she approached the bar.

Most of the men quietly nodded acknowledgement, but only Gordie Alley was brash enough to call back, "Howdy, Georgette, you're sure looking spiffy tonight." The fact is most of the men in The Club were in awe of Georgette. They all knew she was smarter than most of them and she had complete control of her situation. Georgette called the shots. She had first stopped in The Club late one afternoon about a year earlier and had created a sensation. Peg Cavanaugh was the only other reasonably attractive woman who ever came into The Club alone. Some women came in with their husbands and some came in looking for their husbands, but the only other ones who came in alone had good reason to be alone. Even Sammy Griney wouldn't be attracted to them.

Georgette had come in that first night, surveyed the place and had sat down and ordered a beer. All eyes were on her, which didn't seem to bother her a bit as she struck up a conversation with Johnny. She was delighted to find that Johnny was not only articulate but well read and a philosopher. As she talked with Johnny, the courage began to build along the bar and individuals began to remember things they had been meaning to tell Johnny and had not gotten around to doing.

Gordie Alley was the first. He moved closer to where Georgette was sitting and said, "By the way, Johnny, Did I tell you I got the firing pin fixed on that Remington 12 gauge? I was thinking we ought to get out and test fire it."

"Sure, Gordie, anytime. Have you met Georgette here? She drove up from Binghamton. Georgette, this is Gordie Alley." "Pleased to meet you, ma'am," Gordie went into his good old boy routine. "What fetches you all the way out here from the big city?"

"Oh, I just like to drive in the country," said Georgette, who was amused by Gordie's country hick routine and even more amused that he might think she couldn't see through it. "There is so much more individuality to the places than there is in the city. There's such a sameness and predictability to the establishments in the city. And they're not nearly as friendly."

"I've always said that, I have," replied Gordie as he rested one elbow on the bar next to her and turned his back on the gapers, hoping it would help to isolate himself and her from the rest of them.

But it wasn't long before others found reasons to talk to Johnny and to get introduced and much to Gordie's irritation Georgette was soon the center of a casual, pleasant discussion. The conversation was almost entirely between Georgette and Johnny, but every once in awhile one of them would interject a remark he hoped would impress her so that she would single him out for further consideration.

Rhymin' Roy Williams, sizing her up as an educated woman, figured his literary prowess would put him a step or two ahead of the others and he waited for his chance to show her there was a man of letters among these bar hangers.

Johnny was ruminating on the need people have for elbow room, the space to stretch without bopping your neighbor in the nose. "Most of the trouble in this world starts from people living right on top of each other and getting on each others nerves, don't you think?"

"I think you're absolutely right," Georgette said. "We're a claustrophobic society in too many ways."

"I've always said just that thing," interrupted Rhymin' Roy, "What I've always said is 'If you can't stand the kitchen, better stop your bitchin'."

Georgette turned and looked at him quizzically. "Pardon me?"

"Yep, I've always lived by that, 'If you can't stand the kitchen, better stop your bitchin'."

Georgette turned her puzzled expression to Johnny who was doing everything he could to keep from cracking up. He managed to keep a straight face as he said, "Well, now, Roy, I'm not quite sure just how that applies here."

"You got to think about it, Johnny. There's a lot of that symbolism in there. I'm sure Georgette here knows what it means."

Now it was Georgette's turn to keep a straight face. "Well, yes, I believe I do. I must say you have a remarkable choice of metaphors."

Rhymin' Roy was ecstatic. Whatever it was she had said he had a remarkable choice of must have moved him up a notch ahead of the others.

Donkey Nuts Crowley couldn't take any more. "Roy, I don't care what you say, all that bull shit about kitchen and bitchin' don't mean a damn thing. It's just hogwash."

"Hey, come on Donk, watch the language. You're in mixed company here," said Roy, risking an angry Donkey Nuts on the chance it would score him a few more points with this sophisticated lady.

But it did Roy no good that night. As the evening and the conversation wore on it became apparent that Gordie Alley had the inside track. Georgette began to direct more questions and remarks at him until it had become almost a private conversation.

Johnny had become busy behind the bar and only got involved occasionally.

Finally, Georgette got up to leave, waved goodby to everyone and promised to see them again.

As soon as she was out the door, the others converged on Gordie. They demanded to know what he and she had been talking about so long and Gordie just shrugged it off as casual conversation.

"You bastard, I'd like to know what she had to say," said Donkey Nuts. "I wouldn't mind getting some of that."

That started another conversation about her physical attributes that became so animated no one but Johnny noticed Gordie quietly leave.

It wasn't until about an hour later when Gordie returned that they realized something had happened. Gordie was even smugger than his usual smug self and was not about to spill any details except to make it clear that something in fact had happened and that it was something else indeed.

And so the pattern developed that Georgette would occasionally make the drive up from Binghamton, spend a pleasant evening of conversation with Johnny and then select her man of the hour. And there was never any question that it was she who was doing the selecting. Her choice of the evening would wait a judicious 10 minutes after Georgette left and would then slip out to meet her in her car at the edge of town. She had several quiet spots picked out where they wouldn't be disturbed as they consummated their evening liaison.

As time went on they learned that Georgette was married to a moderately wealthy man who she did not care to talk about except to acknowledge that he was an alcoholic who went on periodic binges and who occasionallly beat her black and blue. She was a legal secretary who didn't have to work, but who found it intellectually stimulating. Her husband gave her everything else she wanted, perhaps to make up for the beatings, and she didn't have all that much against him except that he was more interested in making money than in talking to her.

She lived with this for several years until she finally decided she was indeed worthy of more attention and decided to find it on her own. Being the mid-1950s, she couldn't just go bar hopping all over Binghamton where her husband was fairly well known, so she began drifting south into Pennsylvania to the small towns.

She had stopped in several places before she arrived at The Club, but the conversation in most of them didn't get much above the level of what were the best tire chains to use in the snow. It was a pleasant surprise when she found herself discussing the values of life with Johnny. What she found particularly enjoyable about Johnny is that he made observations, not criticisms. His own free-wheeling past made him more tolerant of others' weaknesses. He would have been Georgette's first choice as a back road partner, but she sensed early on that he put too much stock in his recent marriage to gamble it on a one-night stand. He had swum in his share of waters over a good many years and was now content to watch others splash around a bit. It satisfied him to know that if he were interested, Georgette would be, too.

Her visits weren't all that frequent, maybe once or twice a month. And they didn't all end in a dalliance along the road. That just added to the suspense for the hopefuls. Georgette sometimes just wanted to talk and there was no better talker or listener than Johnny. On these nights she would be polite and friendly to everyone but would just as politely turn away their overtures. And so it became a question not only of who she would choose but whether she would choose anyone at all. That added to the suspense for those in the running and, if the truth be told, there was a certain sense of relief among many of them on the nights she chose celibacy because each could feel that he hadn't been rejected in favor of someone else.

One of those who was always in the running when it came to women was Danny Walsh. He had been a lady's man from the day he was reluctantly weaned and had spent most of his teenage years trying to find reasons to unzip his pants. He spent most of his time plotting his next conquest, which for a long time meant plotting his first conquest. He accomplished that one night in the delivery truck he drove for a local grocery. She was a not-so-innocent young thing who convinced Danny he was her first, last and only true love. He didn't realize at that blissful moment that she meant first, last and only as long as he had wheels. He was more concerned at that moment with how you get a five-foot-five-inch frame laid out across the seat of a truck that was only five-feet wide. In his passion, he solved this problem by opening both doors, something he did with some reluctance because it was mid-December.

But he was parked in the cemetery on the hill just outside of town and he figured they wouldn't be exposed to anything more than the elements and it wouldn't take all that long anyway. What he didn't allow for was a sudden snow shower and his woeful lack of knowledge of the female anatomy. By the time he figured out where he was going, how to get there and what to do when he did get there, he had two and a half inches of snow on his frost-bitten ass.

This chilling experience might have soured a lesser soul on love, but not Danny. He just vowed that the next time he would do it sitting up.

He spent his high school years pursuing sports and women, being moderately successful with both. He was a good-looking guy, small but well built with even white teeth and a full head of thick black hair that he spent a good part of his classroom time combing into a perfect DA, or duck's ass, the popular style of the mid 1950s.

He was a dude and a dandy when it came to dressing. He chose his colors carefully, was given to cashmere sleeveless sweaters and always made sure his white bucks were properly scuffed. He was a townie, which made him more of a man about town than the lads who came in off the farm. Along with sports, Danny was also a class leader and was regarded as one of the "in" guys. And trying to get in was pretty much what dominated his life.

He was the horniest little guy around. He was convinced that every girl who so much as looked his way was after his body. "See, see, she's looking right at me!" he would tell his buddy of the moment if a girl even glanced in his direction. "I'm telling ya, she's looking right at me. She wants me to do something."

Chances are the girl would be looking at the clock on the wall to see what time it was, but if the clock was anywhere near Danny, he was convinced it was only an excuse to give him the eye. He would get all excited and become intensely and deadly serious as he plotted how he was going to get next to whatever sweet young thing he was convinced was trying to put the make on him.

One unnerving thing about traveling with Danny is that you always got dragged into his amorous schemes. Girls in the 1950s always traveled in pairs. There were few like Georgette who would venture out alone and it meant that Danny needed a partner to occupy one girl while he made his moves on the other.

Another unnerving thing about traveling with Danny is that he was totally indiscriminate about what he went after. He would pursue a pregnant orangutan as fervently as he would a prom queen. There were none too fat, none too skinny, none to tall, none to short and most distressing for his partner, none too ugly for Danny.

"What do you mean fat?" he would say to his partner. "They're not fat. They're healthy. You don't want to hump a skeleton, do ya?"

"Danny, they can't even sit on the same side of the booth. Look at them. That one looks like Two-Ton Tony Galente."

"OK, OK, I'll take that one then. You take the other one."

"The other one looks like Tony Galente's kid brother."

"God, but you're picky. I'm not asking you to marry them. I just want you to roll around on one of them for a while. You know they say the ones that aren't so good looking are the best. They haven't got much going for them so they work on you-know-what."

"Well, that pair must be the best that ever was then."

"Stop bitchin' will ya? We've got to figure out what we're going to say to them," and Danny would begin an elaborate game plan that as likely as not most of the time would result in not scoring at all, but would occasionally pay off with a few minutes of contortions in the back seat of the contraption of the moment.

After graduating high school, Danny went into the Navy and that made it even worse. He thought no female could resist that bell-bottom uniform and wore it every night he was home. He considered it a magnet that would just draw women to him. One night he and a buddy went to Binghamton looking for some action. They drove into a neighborhood noted for loose women and Danny, decked out in his dress blues, told his buddy to let him out on the corner and to drive around the block. "I'll pick up a couple and when you get back just pull over to the curb. We'll find somewhere to take them."

"Danny, if you pick up anything in this neighborhood, you know what it's going to be. It's going to be the clap, that's what."

"Will you stop worrying and just drive around the block. Just pick us up, that's all."

His partner drove around the block and came back down the street. There stood Danny on the corner, his pea coat collar pulled up against the cold. He was alone. There was no one else on the street. When he saw the car, he furtively motioned his partner to go around again. Another trip around the block and there was Danny on the corner, still all alone and looking colder. He signaled for another circling of the block. Another circle and nothing, only Danny huddled under the street light getting colder by the minute.

After several more trips, he signaled the car over to the curb. He got in and slammed the door. "Let's get the hell out of this god-damned place," he muttered, rubbing his freezing hands together. "It was too cold out, that's what it was."

Incidents like this filled Danny's next few years, but there were also some fertile moments when his efforts paid off and it wasn't always with the Galentes. As a matter of fact, he was successful with some rather attractive selections. It was just that he did not believe in passing up the ugly ones.

Georgette definitely was not one of the ugly ones as Danny sat gazing down The Club bar at some of the finest breastwork he had seen in a long time. Having just returned from the service, Danny had not yet had an encounter with Georgette, but he had heard all about her from his buddy, Hung Houlihan. Hung had filled in Danny on the scenario whenever Georgette paid a visit and Danny was determined to get his shot. He figured that a well-traveled world-wise salty dog like himself should have no trouble with the caliber of Don Juan who frequented The Club.

He had stopped in every day for the two weeks since he had been discharged, but this was the first night Georgette had showed up. It was an evening in early October and just starting to chill down so Georgette was wearing a dark blue fall coat that hung to mid-calf. Danny maintained a look of nonchalance, casting a casual glance her way until she took off the coat. That was the end of the nonchalance. His eyes locked on to a form that was 100 percent form. The lavender knit dress she was wearing climbed up her legs when she slid onto the bar stool. The dress moved with her like another skin. Danny was mesmerized.

There was nothing but three empty bar stools between himself and Georgette, and he had an unobstructed view of the sexiest body he had seen in all his years of carnal pursuit.

Johnny decided to take pity on him and broke his trance by asking him if he wanted another beer. "Huh? Oh, yea, Johnny, I'll have another," Danny said without taking his eyes off Georgette.

"You've been away so long you probably haven't met Georgette here, have you?" Johnny asked.

"Well, no, I can't say that I have and it's been my loss, I'm sure," said Danny, delighted that Johnny had opened the door for him. He had taken note of Gordie Alley's initial greeting to her and figured he had better make his move fast. He decided to go into his Sidney Smooth routine. "What brings a lovely lady like you out to this neck of the woods?"

"Johnny's a friend of mine. I like to stop in and say hello once in awhile."

"Well, I'm ever so glad you decided to stop today. I hope you won't be offended if I say you look like a million dollars in that outfit."

"Now, how could anyone be offended at that kind of remark? I thank you." Georgette was amused by Danny's approach, but couldn't deny enjoying it just the same.

Danny closed the gap between them. "Would it be possible for me to buy you a drink?" he asked.

"It would be if Johnny has any left," Georgette laughed lightly as Danny eased on to the seat next to her. "I haven't seen you here before, have I?"

"No, I've been away serving Uncle Sam for four years. It seems I've been everywhere but home, the South Pacific, California, New England. A lot of traveling, but you learn a little something new everywhere you go."

"Oh, I'm sure you do, it has to be a wonderful education. I've always wanted to travel. It broadens your perspective so much."

"I guess you could say that. It also gives you a wider look at the big picture."

Georgette smiled. They were soon into an easy relaxed conversation. Easy and relaxed for Georgette, that is. Danny, for all his casual chit chat was anguishing over his next move, trying to figure out how he was going to persuade her to share the back seat of a car with him and where it all would be carried out if he did get her to agree.

He also was working himself into a state of paranoia for fear someone else would walk into The Club and turn Georgette's head. He found himself talking almost non-stop to her to keep anyone else from interrupting and he barely nodded acknowledgement to old friends as they arrived during the evening. But worst of all he didn't dare go to the bathroom for fear someone else would move in on him. Georgette wasn't drinking that fast so showed no need to excuse herself, but Danny, in his nervousness, had downed beers almost as steadily as he had been talking.

By mid-evening he was in agony. As Donkey Nuts would have put it, he had to piss like a race horse. He had to go so bad that his stomach began to ache. He kept tightening his groin muscles until he started getting cramps in his ass. Then he would unobtrusively slide one hand into his lap and between his legs and pinch the end of his tool to stem the flow. The urgency in his bladder would ease off for a minute or two and then it would build again.

During all of this excrutiating urinary challenge, Danny managed to keep up a fairly normal conversation with Georgette. He wasn't about to leave her side and allow someone else an opening. He would tie a knot in the end of it first.

Danny was making his way through this mixture of pleasure and pain when Hung Houlihan walked in. 'Damn, damn, damn,' thought Danny. 'Now I'm in real trouble.' Hung was one of Danny's best friends, but he was the last guy he wanted to see right then. Hung attracted women the way honey attracts bees. He was about as laid back, unsophisticated and sloppy as you could get, but women couldn't resist him. He was not a bad-looking guy in a casual way. He was tall and slim with an awkward gait that gave no hint to the fact he was an outstanding athlete. He let his full head of jet black hair flow about any way it wanted to and allowed his clothes to do the same. He could have been described as a casual dresser, but it would be more accurate to call him an indifferent one. Hung was not one to worry about color coding or fit. He selected his clothes by simply taking whatever happened to be on top.

He had an angular face with nicely shaped features except for a nose that tended to sweep up a bit at the end. His real name was Edward Houlihan, but he had been known as Hung since his freshman year of high school when he began to take showers with the basketball team. Nature had provided him with equipment a palomino pony would have envied. Hung was as indifferent about this particular piece of good fortune as he was about everything else. It was there, so make the most of it.

And make the most of it he did. The girls, and later, women were crazy about him. They were crazy about him before a selected number eventually discovered his unique feature. They liked him for the same reason everyone else liked him. He was a genuinely nice guy. Hung loped through life without a care in the world. He was as comfortable talking to Starley Basil as he was the high school principal. And he treated them both the same. Hung did not shift gears when he changed company. And that is what made people comfortable around him. He would do anything for anybody and everybody knew it. Hung's only demand on anyone was that they enjoy themselves, at least in his company.

A particular attraction for women was that Hung never chased them. In high school, the top jocks all went after the prettiest girls and vice versa. They wore their varsity jackets with their letters on them, but Hung, who earned his letter by starting in four sports his freshman year, didn't even own a varsity jacket. His letter was thrown in the back of a drawer somewhere. Hung loved women, but he saw no point in chasing them. If they wanted to come along for the ride, fine. If not, that was fine, too. More often than not they wanted to go along. As a matter of fact, by the time he was out of high school he had so many of them going along that he began giving them nicknames. It would be the Swamp Mare on Monday, Charlotte the Harlot on Tuesday, Bucky Beaver on Wednesday, Flat Bottom on Thursday, and Seven Miles of Bad Road on the weekends. Strangely enough, they were affectionate names as Hung used them, and no offense was taken.

All Danny knew when he saw his old buddy was that he was in danger of losing what he had spent all night cultivating and what, at least for the last hour or two, he had been suffering for. He and Hung would lay down their lives for each other, but when it came to a piece of ass, all bets were off.

"Yo, Danny, how ya doin?" said Hung as he noted Georgette sitting beside him.

"Not bad, Hung, just having a couple of beers." He wasn't about to let Hung know that Georgette had just agreed to meet him down under the viaduct in a few minutes. As a matter of fact, they had been planning their exit when Hung walked in. He didn't even risk letting Hung know he was with Georgette for fear he would want an introduction.

"Hey, what do you say we take a run to Scranton to see what's happening?" asked Hung. "I found a joint down there where they sell beer in schooners and they're only 15 cents."

"Naw, I don't think so. I worked like hell all day and I'm pretty well beat. I think I'm just going to head home and hit the sack," said Danny.

"Come on, I'll drive. Maybe we can do some good down there." Hung knew Danny couldn't pass up a chance at a score.

"Some other time, Hung. I ain't been feelin' right for a couple days now, I don't know what it is, but I can't seem to shake it."

"Well, hell, man, knock down a couple of brandys and haul ass with me. That'll fix you right up."

"Naw, you go ahead. I gotta be up first thing in the morning to go to work on a cottage, and I won't feel for shit if I stay out all night."

"What's the matter with you? You gettin' weak in your old age? Can't you picture what might be waiting down there for us?" Danny's resistance to romance puzzled Hung.

"Maybe this weekend. I just think I'm going to head for home tonight."

When the hell is he going to give up? he thought to himself. By now his bladder was pushing up into his throat and he didn't know if he was even going to be able to get up and walk without leaking all over the floor.

"Well, OK, but it's your loss, old podner," said Hung as he moved on down the bar looking for another sidekick to ride shotgun.

"Yeah, I think I'll head home now," said Danny as casually as a man about ready to burst could say it. Hung nodded goodbye and Danny carefully avoided any eye contact with Georgette so as not to tip anyone to their upcoming rendezvous. He strolled to the door saying good night to everyone, almost sliding his feet along to keep from jarring himself and letting loose a torrent. He was reaching carefully for the door when By God Harry Hollis barged in and banged right into him. Danny rushed past a puzzled Harry and jumped off the steps, tugging frantically at his fly while in midair. He landed next to the building and for a couple of panicky seconds got nowhere with the zipper. But then he got himself free and cut loose a stream with more pressure than a four-inch fire hose. He just kept going and going and was reveling in the pure pleasure of feeling the pressure ease out of his bladder when he heard the giggling behind him. He turned and saw the three little Decker girls tee-heeing and pointing at him.

Mortified, he stuck himself back into his pants and headed quickly and furiously to his car. Georgette had better be good, he fumed.

As he drove down Main Street he could feel the cold night air blowing in under the top of his 1948 Dodge convertible. The top was so ill-fitting that Danny often joked it was warmer with it down than with it up. Making it even colder was the fact the plastic rear window had ripped out and Danny never got around to replacing it. He silently cursed his procrastination as he headed for the viaduct at the north end of town. Georgette had agreed she would wait five to 10 minutes after Danny before leaving The Club and then would meet him under the viaduct where he could join her in her much better insulated brand new Oldsmobile.

The viaduct was a favorite rendezvous location for Danny, and for almost everyone else in Mill Town, for that matter, because it didn't offer just one secluded spot, it offered several. As the road passed under the viaduct, it made a sharp S-curve at either end. And the stone abutments of the viaduct were set back from the road far enough that a car could easily be parked up against either side and barely be seen by someone occupied with negotiating the S curves. By the time a passing motorist noticed a car under the viaduct, he was busy negotiating the S curve going out the other end. The S curves also provided little offshoots that banked down below road level so that a car parked on them could barely be seen by someone driving by. The viaduct was a perfect place for extracurricular activity and the evidence of that littered the ground under it. There was more used rubber under the viaduct than there was at the Five-Mile Point Speedway.

Danny pulled under the viaduct and shut off the motor. It didn't do much good to keep the car running because the heat just leaked out through the top as fast as the heater could throw it out. Danny thought to play the radio, but decided he better not take a chance on running down the battery so he sat in shivering silence hoping Georgette didn't dilly dally.

He was still hoping 15 minutes later as he occupied himself trying to blow smoke rings with the frost from his breath. The wind was funneling under the viaduct and Danny had parked with his back to it, which meant, of course, that it was whistling right in through the rear window. He slouched down in the driver's seat with his hands deep in his pockets and his head pulled down into his jacket as far as he could get it. He consoled himself by visualizing how Georgette was going to thaw the chill that was taking over his body.

A half hour passed and Danny was beginning to get annoyed. He also was beginning to realize that there was only one part of him that wasn't as stiff as a board. He sat there like a cardboard cutout because every time he moved, it made him aware of how cold he was. Maybe Georgette didn't know how to find the viaduct. But, no, she had assured him she knew exactly were it was. A less amorous soul would have given up long since, but when Danny Walsh was in rut, which was all the time, a Yukon freeze wouldn't deter him from accomplishing his goal or trying to accomplish it.

Forty-five minutes had passed and even Danny was beginning to weigh the advantages of life without sex. No anxiety about being turned down, no emotional scars from a broken relationship, no wasted hours of pleading and begging, no money wasted on drinks and trinkets. And no freezing your balls off under a viaduct.

He was doing his best to shake those insane thoughts out of his head when he saw the headlights sweep around the curve. "This is it!" he thought as the warm feeling of passion ran over him like water from a hot shower. Time for old Danny boy to do some good.

The car slowed down as it came under the viaduct and Danny opened his door to make his transfer. But the car didn't stop. It moved slowly on through the viaduct and eased off the shoulder to where it was almost hidden in some shrubs. "Must be she really likes her privacy," Danny thought to himself as he made his way up to the car. He reached the back of the car and was moving around to the passenger side when he heard voices. He couldn't see because the windows were all steamed up. But he did hear Georgette exclaim, "My, my, you really are a piece of work."

A couple of grunts and then, "and you ain't a bit bad yourself. You realize that if old Danny hadn't been feeling so lousy tonight, I'd probably be all the way to Scranton by now."

IT'S ALL A MATTER OF HONOR

"WHAT WE GOT TO do is we got to kick some ass. We got to beat some respect into them."

Gordie Alley was not a happy man. He had made the mistake of stopping into the Big Bend Grill for a beer on his way home from work and had encountered just about the entire Big Bend Grill softball team all dressed up in their red and white uniforms. There was no love lost between Gordie and anyone on the Big Bend Grill softball team.

In fact, there was no love lost between anyone from Mill Town and anyone from Big Bend. The two boroughs had been at war with each other for the 200 years since Jacob Hallstead had built a cabin and a makeshift ferry on a sweeping bend of the Susquehanna River and Gaylord Whitney had carried his meager belongings down from Connecticut and had thrown up a one-man sawmill along what was later named Salt Lick Creek in the prettiest valley of the rolling hills of what was to become Susquehanna County.

The two settlements were five miles apart and even back then they were five miles too close to each other. Despite the fact they were only an hour's ride from each other, Jacob Hallstead and Gaylord Whitney didn't exchange words more than four or five times a year. They spent most of the time in between spying on each other. Gaylord would make his way along the east ridge of the valley to a spot overlooking Jacob's homestead at the same time Jacob was making his way along the west ridge of the valley to a spot where he would have a full view of Gaylord's sawmill. They would lie in the grass for hours watching for any telltale signs of suspicious movement, ignorant of the fact the other guy was five miles behind him looking the other way.

Jacob and Gaylord might not have been aware of the other's spying activities, but the Indians were perfectly aware of what each of them was doing all the time. It didn't take them long to make the most of the settlers' suspicious natures. For some reason the Indians didn't bother to try to figure out, Jacob and Gaylord always seemed to pick the same time to go spy on each other. Indian sentries assigned to each of the sites would stoke up their signal fires as soon as the two men had lit out through the woods. By the time Jacob and Gaylord were half way to their destinations, Indian parties would be in each of their camps making off with anything they could carry or drag.

After several hours of guard duty, the two settlers would return to their respective dwellings only to find that they had been ripped off. Not having caught even a glimpse of each other during their vigils, each naturally assumed the other had raided his camp while he was away. This continued on a more or less regular basis for several years with neither of them having the sense or the courage to confront the other about the thievery. The Indians, on the other hand, gave up trying to scratch a living out of the rock-infested land and contented themselves by helping themselves to Jacob's and Gaylord's groceries whenever the two of them set out on a mission.

Jacob and Gaylord eventually managed to acquire a couple of hapless wives to share their frontier misery and with not much else to entertain themselves, they began producing offspring. Their spying days and the Indian raids petered out. They, of course, passed their animosity toward each other on to their children and anyone else who happened to settle in their respective communities and by the time Gordie Alley encountered the Big Bend Grill softball team on that Aug. 5 evening of 1955, he was also encountering an antagonism that had survived and thrived for almost two centuries.

Gordie, like a good many other courageous and reasonably obnoxious Mill Town males, had had his run-ins with the Big Bend contingent at dances and other sporting events. It was a feather in the cap of any Mill Town lad who could make time with a girl from Big Bend and it was a frequent attempt because the Mill Town girls weren't all that much to write home about. The Big Bend bunch, on the other hand, viewing the female situation from an entirely different perspective, saw hometown pickings as slim indeed, but viewed the Mill Town lasses as exciting and mysterious. Another mystery that remained unchallenged, unquestioned and unexplored but readily accepted over the years is that it was easier to score with a girl from the other town. And so the young bucks from Mill Town kept showing up at dances in Big Bend and vice versa sniffing around the skirted prospects while keeping a close eye out for trouble. Many a young man got his first dance and his first black eye on the same night. Sporting events provided even greater opportunity for mayhem. Baseball, basketball and first degree assault were the primary sports of the time and they were followed closely and violently by even the older people in the two towns. Many were the basketball games between them that ended up with only a couple or three player still on the court at game's end because of fouls and injuries.

And budding young pitchers spent much more time working on their bean ball than they did their fastball or curve. Getting the book on an opposing hitter didn't mean learning whether he could hit the fastball or curve. It meant learning which way he ducked.

And so it was with this history of ill feeling that Gordie Alley stomped into The Club and declared it was time to bring the Big Bend Grill softball team to its collective knees.

"We're going to whip those bastards so bad they'll dig a hole and pull it in on top of them. They won't dare to show their faces for a week."

"What did they do to you this time, Gordie? Did they paint your dobber red or something?" asked Donkey Nuts, who always got a kick out of seeing Gordie in an uproar.

"Listen, this ain't funny, Donk. Those sons of bitches claimed we never had a team in this town that could give them a run for their money and you know what else they said? Wait till you here this. They said you weren't the best left-handed hitter to come out of this county. How do you like that shit?"

Donkey Nuts didn't like it one bit nor did anyone else in The Club. The place erupted with curses, oaths and vows of vengeance. It was one thing to sneak in and make out with Mill Town women, but to even kiddingly assert that Donkey Nuts was not the greatest left-handed hitter in Susquehanna County history was beyond the beyond.

"Just who the hell do they think they are to say a thing like that? Who do they think was any better?" asked Glen Tink.

"They claim Goosey Parker was better," said Gordie.

"Goosey Parker! That fat bastard couldn't hit a cow with a snow shovel. Even if he did hit it they would have to truck him down to first base in a wheel barrow." Hung Houlihan was getting into it.

"By God, in my day there wasn't nobody in that whole damn town could match up with our team," declared a thick-voiced By God Harry Hollis as he nursed a quart of Stegmaiers he hoped would ease him down off his three-day spree. "They wouldn't dare say the things Gordie said they said…" and By God Harry lost his train of thought and his voice trailed off.

"You're right there, By God," said Henry Wabash firmly. "We cleaned their clock every time we played them." Neither By God Harry nor Henry had ever so much as swung a bat in an organized contest, but that didn't matter. It was a case of we against them no matter if you were the star hitter Donkey Nuts or the 80-year-old telephone operator Delia Arney. It was town against town and there was no room for middle-of-the-roaders. "Gordie is right. We've got to come up with a way to wipe their noses and stick their hankies in their pockets," said Johnny who was beginning to get into it as much as his customers. "And it's got to be something they're not going to be able to forget for awhile."

"I already took care of that," said Gordie. "I challenged the Big Bend Grill to a softball game." "You did what!" exclaimed Glen Tink. "I thought you meant we were going to go down there and beat on their heads. That's damn near a pro team. How the hell are we supposed to beat them? Those guys practice three nights a week for God's sake."

"Yeah, and they've got Gene Doolan pitchin' for them," said Hung. "He pitches in three fast-pitch leagues in Binghamton. There ain't nobody can hit him. He's got a whole shit load of no-hitters."

"Well, we can practice, too, can't we?" Gordie said defensively. "Most of you guys have played some baseball. Some of you are still playing."

Hung, who was one of the better baseball players ever to come out of Mill Town and who still played for a bar in Binghamton, tried to explain to Gordie that there is no relationship to hitting a baseball no matter how hard it is thrown and trying to hit a fast-pitch softball that does everything but write "You're out" when issued up by a talented windmill pitcher.

"Gordie, you can't even see the damn thing. You have to start swinging when he goes into his windup and hope you guessed the right spot."

Gordie, who had played plenty of baseball and had played it well, had never seen a fast-pitch softball. "What the hell, the damn ball is twice as big as a baseball. How the hell hard can it be to hit it?"

"I'm telling you Gordie, If Doolan is on, his infield could go off in the bushes and screw and he wouldn't have anything to worry about. We wouldn't be able to touch him. We have to find a different way to show these guys up."

"We can't do that, Hung," Gordie said hesitantly and he began to fidget as he glanced at the others. "I already made a bet with them."

"A bet? What did you do, go and bet them a keg of beer? Dammit, Gordie, why do you always have to shoot your mouth off," said Hung. "You telling me we've got to buy beer for them bastards?"

"No, I didn't bet them a beer, I bet them something else." "What?"

"Well, you got to let me explain how it happened." Gordie was not a bit comfortable as the others gathered around. He was feeling more apprehensive by the minute.

"Let's hear it, Gordie," said Donkey Nuts in a threatening tone. "Well, I was drinkin' some, you see, and they were mouthin' off something awful. You know how those guys are and they all started to gang up on me and kept making fun of everything in Mill Town and saying that we didn't have a softball team because there wasn't anything but girls living in this town and that they knew that for a fact because they'd plugged every one of them and that the reason they were so easy to plug is that there weren't no men in town to take care of them and they kept that up until I was startin' to get a a little steamed. And then they said that about Donk not being the best hitter and I really got pissed."

"So I told them that I had just drove through Big Bend and didn't see nothin' but pussies on the street and I figured their softball team must be pussies too."

"Atta boy, Gordie, and what did they say then?"

"Well, a couple of them started to come at me but Don Gilles stopped them and said he didn't want any fightin' in his bar but he had a way to settle it. He said that as long as we were so fired up to call each other pussies that we ought to once and for all prove which ones really were. He said we should play five innings and whichever team was ahead then was the men and the one behind was the girls."

"So we play five innings. So what's the bet?" said Donkey Nuts.

"Well, Don said the team that's behind after five innings has got to change and play the rest of the game dressed like girls." The Club exploded.

"Are you out of your mind!" shouted Houlihan. "What the hell is the matter with your head. Good God, man, we can't do that." "Gordie, you have got to be about the dumbest son of a bitch that ever walked," said Donkey Nuts. "You ain't got the brains God gave a piss ant."

"I ain't dressin' up like no girl," said Glenn Tink. "Bullshit on that nonsense."

The uproar continued with a selection of oaths and profanities and references to Gordie Alley's intelligence that did not put him right up there with Einstein or even Mortimer Snerd. They were all talking at once and the only thing you could establish from the babble was that no way in God's whole world were any of them going to be caught dead wearing a dress.

"You wouldn't really have to wear a dress," Gordie said when he could finally get a word in.

"Oh, you mean you was just kidding?"

"Well, no, but the bet wasn't about dresses. It was about underwear."

"Just what the hell are you talking about?"

"The losing team has to dress up in women's underwear."

The place really went wild then. Nobody was listening to anybody else. Everyone was spitting expletives as fast as they could think of them. Gordie began to feel more threatened than he did in the Big Bend Grill.

"Gordie," said Johnny, "I've known your mother and your father for 32 years and, nice as they are, I've never considered either one of them to have much of a think tank. But never in my whole life did I think they were dumb enough to sire a complete imbecile."

Others didn't bother to articulate quite so carefully.

"You are a bonafide fool."

"You ain't got no hay in your mow, man."

"You are a certified crazy bastard."

"Your ass sucks well water."

"You'd fart in church and blame it on the angels."

"Did your ma have any kids that lived?"

Gordie was beginning to feel offended. He realized that he may have overcommitted in an alcohol-weakened moment, but he didn't think it was reason enough for the whole town to turn on him. What made it even worse was that, as best he could remember, he hadn't only made the bet, he had made it in writing. At least he remembered signing some kind of document that Don Gilles had drawn up. So he began doing what he did best. Bullshitting.

"Now wait a minute. You're acting like we already lost the game. We ain't lost nothin' and we ain't goin' to lose nothin'. You all think I'm so damn dumb. Well, I'll show you how dumb I am. I happen to know for a fact that Gene Doolan isn't going to be pitchin' for them."

That slowed the menacing conversation.

"What are you trying to say, Gordie?"

"I'm saying I know that Doolan got his draft notice and has already gone for his physical. He's in the same bunch with my cousin and my cousin says he's got to report to Wilkes-Barre to get sworn in a week from Wednesday. We don't play till that next Saturday and Doolan will be scrubbin' latrines in Fort Dix by then.

"Goddamn it, Gordie, are you sure?" asked Donkey Nuts.

"You think I'd lie to you. Sure, I'm sure. We ain't got nothin' to worry about. The rest of the guys on the team are just a bunch of stumblebums."

"Wait a minute, Gordie, if Doolan is going in the Army, how come Don Gilles doesn't know about it?" asked Johnny. "Gilles wouldn't make a bet unless he was damn sure of winning."

"I don't know, Johnny. Maybe Doolan hasn't said anything to him. Gilles has been paying him 20 bucks a game. Maybe he was afraid Gilles would get another pitcher if he knew he was leaving. All I know is my cousin was right there with him on the bus when they went for their physicals." That part was true. His cousin had said he had seen Doolan on the same bus and he had seen Doolan going into the induction center and he had seen him standing there in his skivvies waiting to be weighed and his cousin had received his notice to appear for induction so it only made sense that Doolan was going, too. At any rate it was the best Gordie had to work with to get the irate crowd off his back and on his side.

He continued his sales pitch. "Can't you just see those fruits out there running around in brassieres and panties?" he said to a once more interested group. "Just imagine Boonie Wilson trying to stuff his fat ass into one of them panty girdles."

"Yeah, and I can just see Boney Newhouse prancin' around out there in a garter belt and stockings. I always thought he looked a little queer," said Houlihan.

"What I'd like to see is that stuck up snob-nosed Carl Hinkle out there in a pair of bloomers," said Danny Walsh. "I owe that turd from basketball."

In no time, Gordie had not only managed to extricate himself from a bad situation, but had also turned it around to where he had everyone in The Club picturing his favorite enemy on the Big Bend team decked out in women's undies.

"Let's not get too carried away," cautioned Johnny. "Remember, these guys have been playing right along. You guys haven't lifted a bat in a coon's age."

"Danny and Donk and Hung and me have been playing baseball," said Gordie. "We ought to be able to handle a big old softball. What we got to do is get everybody up to the playground for practice. We're going to have to line up some more guys, too. By God Harry, Henry and Shake ain't going to be able to play a whole game. They're going to have to be subs."

By God Harry, Henry and Shake Ketter weren't too happy about Gordie's assessment of their stamina, but had to admit they were in no shape to be running around a ball diamond for nine innings.

"Tink can play and so can Willard and Emery. Rhymin' Roy has played before, too," said Hung. "And we can probably pick up a couple of guys from our old town team. If they can play baseball, they can learn softball."

"Now wait just a god-damned minute," squeaked Sammy. "What about me? You forget about me?"

"You can be the bat boy," Gordie replied.

"Bat boy, my ass!" Sammy was furious. "I can play as good as the rest of these guys. What, have you got to be seven feet tall to play on this team? I know how to play this game."

"When did you ever play softball?" Gordie wanted to know.

"I played when I was in school, that's when."

"Good God, you're talking about on the playground at recess," Gordie said. "Even the girls played then."

"So what? It's all the same thing. You got to hit and catch the ball."

"Let's just wait and see, OK?" said Gordie to get the indignant little man off his back. "I'll put you down and we'll see how many guys we have."

"Do I get a uniform?" Sammy was insistent.

"What do you mean, a uniform? None of us has uniforms," said Gordie.

"What kind of a raggedy-ass team we gonna look like without uniforms?" Sammy wanted to know.

"Sammy's right, Gordie," said Hung. "We'd look a helluva lot better if we were all dressed alike. It'd be a lot more professional than just finding any old damn thing to wear."

"Where am I supposed to get uniforms? I can't afford to buy uniforms." Gordie was beginning to feel a bit burdened by it all.

"I'll tell you what," said Johnny. "I'll spring for shirts as long as you promise not to put my name on them. I don't want everybody thinking they can put the bite on me to sponsor something." The truth was that Johnny was not at all sure of the outcome of the upcoming contest and did not want his establishment's name permanently attached to what could become the greatest humiliation in Susquehanna County history. "Your place don't really have a name anyway," Sammy pointed out. It was true. There was no sign on the drab old building to indicate any particular ownership, just a couple of neon signs assuring you what kind of beer you could find within. The Club was just an affectionate name Hung and Danny had come up with one night and others had begun to use it. Most people simply said "I'm going to go see Johnny" when referring to their destination.

"Be that as it may, I just don't want you guys running around with my name on your shirt attracting everybody that's trying to get a bowling team or something started."

"Well, what shall we call ourselves then?" asked Gordie. This whole thing was getting to be more responsibility than Gordie had ever intended to assume in his entire life. "If only I hadn't had to take that piss, I'd have gone right by the Big Bend Grill," he groused to himself.

"I got a name for us," said Rhymin' Roy, "Let's call ourselves the Amazin' Cajuns."

"The Amazin' Cajuns? What in God's name is that supposed to mean?" asked Donkey Nuts.

"Ain't Cajuns some kind of Indians down south that play accordions?" asked Sammy.

"Yeah, they got something to do with that Hank Williams song about feeling up gumbo or something like that," said Hung.

"But what the hell does it have to do with us?" asked Donkey Nuts.

"Look, it rhymes don't it? What else do you want?" Rhymin' Roy's artistic temperament was being pinged.

"Well, I know what I don't want. I don't want to go around being named after some accordion-playing Indian," said Donkey Nuts.

"All right, don't worry about it, I'll come up with another name," said Gordie. He got paper and pen from Johnny and started writing down the names of players so he would know how many shirts to order. As he was doing that, Peg Cavanaugh walked into The Club.

"Hey, boys, what's up, and with you, Sammy, I'm sure it ain't much."

"Oh, yeah, How would you know?" was Sammy's best effort to silence the laughter.

"Just an educated guess and you can bet your sweet ass that's all it's ever going to be," said Peg. Sammy had lost as usual.

"Hey, Peg, we're getting up a softball team to play Big Bend. You interested?" asked Willard.

"Naw, girl's don't play softball," said Peg.

"I know, but are YOU interested?" asked Willard.

"Why you friggin' little ..." Peg made a menacing move as Willard slid behind Donkey Nuts.

"Wait a minute, Peg, you can be our cheerleader," said Johnny. "It will give this team a touch of class."

"Hey, you know, you're right, that might be fun. What's Sammy going to be, the team mascot? Maybe we could put a collar on him and lead him around the field before the game."

"Oh yeah? Well, you ought to be on a basketball team. You're carrying two of them around with you all the time," said Sammy.

At last. Sammy had scored and the whole place let him know it. Even Peg just went over and threw an affectionate headlock on him and pulled him into her enormous chest. "Oh, yeah, well dribble these," she said and the place exploded.

The next night after work, everyone who could showed up at the school ballfield. If Gordie had any thoughts of beating Big Bend they quickly dissolved when his players took the field for batting practice. Henry Wabash was on the mound with a half dozen warped softballs scattered around him and Shake Ketter was at the plate swinging a bat menacingly. Henry underhanded a dozen pitches not one of which made it to the plate in the air and four of which swooped up into the sky and plopped in the dust about three feet in front of him.

"Come on, Henry, get it over so he can hit it," said Danny.

"I'm just finding my range, I don't want to give him nothin' too good," said Henry.

"For God's sake, it's batting practice, he's supposed to hit it," yelled Danny.

After a couple of dozen more pitches, Henry started getting the ball over the plate, but Shake wasn't having any part of it. He never lifted the bat from his shoulder.

"Shake, what the hell are you doin'? Hit the ball," ordered Gordie from behind the backstop.

"I'm waiting for my pitch," said Shake, eyeing Henry intensely, "Well, wait for it over by the dugout," said Gordie. "Donk, you get in and hit a few." Shake grudgingly relinquished the plate to Donkey Nuts.

The man was something to see swinging a bat. His sloping muscular form wound the bat around behind him and cocked it there, his powerful hands strangling the bat handle.

When he swung, it was with a smooth extended motion that put every ounce of his body behind the bat. His follow through brought him almost all the way around. He pounded ball after ball down the right field line over the running track and into an adjacent field. Those who weren't chasing the fly balls watched in admiration.

After Donkey Nuts had finished, everyone else took turns hitting a few. Henry had long since been banished to the outfield and Gordie had taken over on the mound so things moved along at a faster pace.

Danny, Hung and Emery had provided Gordie with a few moments of positive thinking, but the rest of the lineup quickly dispelled any notion he might have had of fielding a pennant winner. Willard spent most of his time fouling the ball off his left foot and hopping around on his right one bellowing in pain. Shake Ketter stepped back in and took a dozen pitches right down the middle without offering at any of them. When Gordie asked him what the hell he was doing, he said he was looking for the high hard one.

By God Harry was probably the most distressing feature in the team's shaky offense. He stood at the plate, coveralls and all, and swung at every pitch that came up no matter where it was. If it rolled across the plate, he swung at it. If it was three feet over his head, he swung at it. He swung at two that were thrown behind him. The problem was he swung the bat in the same spot every time. He had a vicious waist high cut that never varied up or down. The only way it varied was that he often swung before the ball got there or after it went by, but his location was as consistent as could be. About five quarts of booze had trickled out of his pores in the warm evening sun before he finally stepped out of the box without once laying wood to a single pitch. "I gotta work on my timing," he concluded.

Glen Tink's hitting was not nearly as annoying to Gordie as it was to Rhymin' Roy who was catching. Despite his pipe cleaner frame, Tink fancied himself a power hitter. He wound himself up like a clock spring on every pitch and came whipping back around with so much effort that he exploded in a loud grunt. Much to Rhymin' Roy's dismay, this enormous physical effort also forced a loud fart out of him each time. Roy squatted behind Tink through a half dozen series of grunt-fart, grunt-fart, grunt-fart until his nose and eyes could take it no longer. He threw his mitt down in disgust. "Jesus, Glen, but you're foul," he said, rubbing his eyes. "Put a cork in it, will ya?"

Tink turned the tables on Roy. "Well, you know what they say, Roy, No pain, no gain."

Infield practice might have gone better if it had not been for Sammy. Gordie had Hung on third, Danny at short and Tink at second, all reasonably decent infielders. But Sammy had arrived at practice with an old, moth-eaten first base mitt he had fished out of the attic and had insisted that was his position.

"Don't give me that shit, Sam," Gordie told him. "First basemen are supposed to be tall and left-handed."

"That ain't so," said Sammy. "Besides, it's the only glove I got."

"Well, let Willard use it and go out in the outfield," said Gordie.

"No sir. Ain't nobody using this glove but me and I got a right to try out at first if I got the only first-base glove," Sammy insisted. "Then get the hell out there and try it, but you better know how to use it," Gordie said testily.

Sammy's woeful lack of knowledge about playing first base became evident as soon as he reached the position. He promptly stepped up on to the bag and stood there like a statue facing second. It added two inches to his height, but considerably cut down on his mobility.

Gordie, who was at home plate with a bat in his hand ready to hit ground balls to the infield, called out, "Sammy, what are you doing?"

Sammy turned to look at him but remained standing on the bag.

"I'm playing first base, what does it look like?"

"It looks like you're imitating General Sherman in the park. You're not supposed to stand on the bag like that. You're supposed to get off it and down the baseline a little. Be ready for action."

"Look, you're goin' to hit the ball down to one of these guys and they're goin' to pick it up and throw it over here and sooner or later I gotta be on this bag to catch it if I'm goin' to get anybody out so why should I be runnin ' all over the place when I can be here already before they even throw it?" Sammy reasoned.

Gordie bowed his head. "We ain't got a chance in hell," he said quietly. But not one to give up, he turned to Hung on third. "Get one," he said and hit a sharp ground ball that Hung gobbled up cleanly and fired on a line to first. It was a perfect throw that would have hit the average first baseman right in the chest. But it was a foot over Sammy's head and, therefore, as far as Sammy was concerned, out of reach. He never even raised his glove and it went sailing into the creek behind him.

"What the hell was the matter with that? It was right to you," Gordie screamed.

"It was not. It was a wild throw. I don't have no stepladder over here, you know."

"Oh, my God," Gordie groaned as he hit one down to short. "Get one, Danny." Danny picked up the ball on one hop and, mindful of Hung's mistake, threw low to first. The ball came in at Sammy's shoetops and, as a matter of fact, hit him right on the big toe, but he never made a move for it. He yelped as the ball ricocheted off into the grass, but remained on the bag.

"Now, tell me that friggin' throw was too high," Gordie raged. "No, it wasn't too high. You could see it wasn't too high. It was too damn low. What am I supposed to do get a shovel and dig them out of the ground?" Sammy said defiantly.

"This ain't goin' to work," Gordie moaned as he picked up another ball. His problems with Sammy were taken care of a couple of minutes later when it was Sammy's turn to field one. "It's comin' at you," Gordie said darkly, but Sammy remained riveted to the bag. Gordie stopped. "You gotta get off the damned bag if you're goin' to field the ball," he said.

"Why should I get off the bag until I know where it's goin? It might come right here," said Sammy.

"I'm goin' to knock that little bastard right on his ass," Gordie muttered to himself and swung at the ball as hard as he could. Instead of hitting a scorching grounder at Sammy, he got under it and popped it high into the air. Sammy finally left the bag. "I got it! I got it!" he yelled and began running around the right side of the infield trying to get a bead on the ball that was still heading up into the clouds. Gordie had really tagged it. Sammy ran toward home plate, then back peddled toward first, then swerved sideways toward the pitcher's mound where he tripped on the rubber and almost fell down. He then ran backwards toward second and crab walked sideways toward first again, all the time keeping his head locked back and his eyes on the sky.

He finally figured he was under the ball and reached up for it with both arms. But it seemed to him that it was never going to come down and he decided for some insane reason to go up after it. He bent his little legs and jumped as high as he could, which was about six inches above the ground. He was going up just as the ball was coming into his range and in the excitement of the moment he forgot to use his glove. The ball rocketed down cleanly between his upstretched arms and didn't touch a thing until it reached his left eye. It nailed Sammy with a splat that made everyone in the infield a little queasy. By the time Sammy's feet had returned to earth, his left eye was blown up and closed tighter than Petey Slater's wallet. He never uttered a sound. He wobbled forward a couple of steps then backwards before quietly keeling over on his back like a fallen plank. He lay there stunned with his one good eye staring into the sun.

Gordie walked over and tugged the glove off his hand and tossed it to Willard. "I told you first basemen were supposed to be tall," he said to the prone figure as he headed back to home plate to hit another round to the infield.

The team practiced every night for a week, many of them forgoing their dinners in their determination to get in as much workout as they could. They practiced until it became so dark they had to hear the ball rather than see it. When Gordie would decide it was just getting too dangerous he would reluctantly call it off and they would all head for The Club.

As game day approached, Gordie assessed the situation and decided they just might have a chance of winning. He had a fairly solid defense now that Sammy was off first and without Doolan to blow the ball by them, he figured his hitters should be able to get him some runs. He had spent hours by himself practicing pitching against the side of the barn and had gotten to where he could consistently whip a screamer into a circle he had painted on the door.

The game was scheduled for 5 o'clock on a Wednesday afternoon and the team gathered at The Club to get their game shirts and so they could all drive to Big Bend together as a demonstration of team unity and strength. Gordie set the box of new shirts on the bar and ripped it open. "We only got one size so you're just going to have to fit into them," he said as he began pulling them out. He handed one to Hung who gazed at it in admiration. The shirts were black with shiny white numbers front and back. Hung turned his around and looked at the back as Gordie was handing shirts to the others.

"What the hell is this name on the back?" he asked.

"That's our team name," said Gordie, "I figured the Hitters was a good strong name."

"This don't say Hitters. This says Shitters," said Hung.

"So does mine," said By God Harry. It didn't take long to discover that all the shirts said Shitters.

"Dammit, I knew I should have written it down for him. That guy didn't look like he knew how to spell cat," groaned Gordie. "Well, we're going to have to wear them. Maybe nobody will notice." "Not notice! How the hell they not goin' to notice when we're standin' out there in front of them all night long?" Donkey Nuts was in his usual good mood.

"Well, just keep movin' so they can't read it so easy," said Gordie.

"Sure, I'm goin' to keep jumpin' up and down all night so they can't read my shirt? Good God," said Donkey Nuts.

"I don't care what you do about it, we got to wear them so we can at least look like a team," Gordie said. "Now, let's get goin' so we can get some practice in before the game."

"What do you say boys, how do I look?" Peg had gone into the men's room and put on her shirt.

"Jesus to Jesus!" gasped Willard as he stared at two huge white zeroes perfectly circling Peg's eye-popping breasts. The shirt was stretched to its seam-threatening limits.

"I thought that would be a good number for you," said Gordie with a grin. No one disagreed.

They all went out and piled into Gordie's and Tink's pickup trucks with most of them riding in back and headed off for Big Bend.

Big Bend had gone in for softball in a big way and had built a regulation softball diamond on the edge of town complete with an outfield fence covered with advertisements. They also had several rows of bleachers that were beginning to fill up by the time the Shitters arrived. Everyone in Big Bend and Mill Town knew about the game and knew what was at stake and nobody was about to miss it.

Gordie and Tink had hardly killed the engines on the pickups when everyone in back started talking at once.

"Do you see what I see?"

"What is this shit?"

"Holy Christ, what went wrong?"

"We are down the toilet for sure."

There on the Big Bend side of the field was Gene Doolan warming up. Warming up was hardly the word for it. He was blazing pitches that his catcher could hardly hang onto. The ball dipped, hooked, dropped and climbed in the fraction of the second it took to leave Doolan's long skinny arm and smack into the catcher's mitt.

One pitch would scream to the plate almost too fast to see. The next would flutter around like a ping pong ball in a strong wind.

The Shitters stood there staring at this pitching phenomenon and a bad feeling ran through all of them. Doolan was not cleaning latrines at Fort Dix and their asses were grass. They quickly converged on Gordie and backed him up against the side of his pickup.

"Let's hear it, shit for brains. How do you explain this?" Donkey Nuts demanded. The rest of them echoed his question in terms not quite so endearing.

"I don't know what happened," wailed Gordie feeling very much maligned, put upon and persecuted. He was also feeling slightly claustrophobic as his own players wedged him against the door of his truck. "Maybe there is something wrong with him."

"By God, he looks healthy enough to me," said By God Harry as Doolan rifled a pitch that almost knocked his catcher down.

"Well, we don't have much choice now," said Hung. "We got to play these bastards. But I'll tell ya, Gordie, If we lose, you're goin' to have every right to wear women's bloomers 'cause we're goin' to cut your balls off."

Gordie winced and squeezed his knees together.

The Shitters took the field for practice and they had the entire crowd wondering why they were running backwards and sideways out on to the field. Nobody really got wise until Rhymin' Roy stepped in to catch. He stood facing the backstop with his back to the mound as long as he could, but he began to feel rather foolish staring into the faces of the fans and realized that Gordie was never going to get any warmups unless he turned around. So he turned and faced the field. No one noticed anything for about 30 seconds. Then a 10-year-old spelling champ said, "Look, mom, he's got Shitters on his back."

The word buzzed through the stands and in no time the place was in an uproar. The Big Bend fans were going wild and the Mill Town fans were doing their best to sink down into their wooden seats.

Practice finally ended and the two paid umpires brought in from Scranton called the team managers together. Gordie and Don Gilles told the umpires about the bet and Gilles explained that he had an assortment of ladies undergarments, more than enough to outfit a team, in the back of his station wagon. He flashed the signed bet under Gordie's nose with a smirk and showed it to the umps. They shook their heads in amazement and promised to halt the game at the end of the fifth inning for the appropriate change of uniforms.

Gilles was feeling rather good about things after watching the Shitters practice and he said, "I'll tell you what, Gordie. Just to make it more interesting, we'll stop after the seventh inning, too, and whoever's behind will have to wear the ladies duds. How's that? Give you half a chance."

Gordie said it didn't matter to him. At that point he couldn't see where it would make any difference anyway. As Gilles started back to his bench, Gordie grabbed his arm.

"I thought Doolan was supposed to go in the Army last week. What the hell is he doing here?"

"Didn't you hear about that? It's a riot," Gilles said. "He breezed through his physical with no problems and then they did that psychological stuff on him. You know, that stuff about do you hate your father and all that? Well,

Doolan was all hung over from his going away party the night before and things weren't coming through too good for him. When the guy asked him if he liked boys, he thought he said 'Do you like toys?' And he said, yeah, that he used to take all kinds of them to bed with him. And then he said that now that he's older, he doesn't want anyone to see him so he only plays with them out behind the barn. And then the guy asked him did he like girls and Doolan got it screwed up again and thought he said 'Do you like squirrels?' and he said that he had never tried to eat one, but he didn't think he would care to. And he said the only thing he had ever had to do with them was to shoot at a couple that was trying to get into his house. Well, that did it for old Doolan. He was back home on the next bus."

"You mean they let him out because they thought he was a fairy? He's tapped half the girls in Mill Town," Gordie said.

"I know it," said Gilles. "But, like I say, he wasn't in very good shape that day and didn't know what the hell was going on. He's mortified about the whole thing. Says he's going to try to get them to give him the test over. But that ain't going to do you any good because he's here now and sharper than a tack."

He didn't have to tell Gordie that. Gordie could see him warming up. He returned glumly to his bench and announced his lineup. He was pitching. Rhymin' Roy was catching, Hung was on third, Danny on short, Tink on second, Willard on first, Emery in left, Donkey Nuts in centerfield and By God Harry in right.

Shake Ketter was his roving fielder and Sammy his first sub off the bench. He had Tink leading off. "C'mon Glen, get this thing rolling," Gordie called out as Tink stepped in to the box. Doolan reared back and cut loose with a fast ball right down the middle. Tink never got the bat off his shoulder. In fact, he thought it was a trick play where Doolan faked the pitch and the catcher had the ball all the time. But when the ump hollered strike, he realized how foolish that thought was and hunkered down for the next pitch. Doolan's next offering came blazing in below Tink's knees but about four feet in front of the plate it suddenly dipped up and came right in on the letters. Tink stood there with his mouth open and it was still open when he heard strike three splat into the catcher's mitt a minute later. He returned to the bench in a daze.

Doolan quickly dispensed with Danny and Hung, two of George's best hitters, and things were not looking too good for the Shitters. They took the field and Gordie's practice pitching against the barn paid off. He had enough on it that he was able to keep Big Bend from getting good wood on the ball and got them out in order.

Donkey Nuts was hitting cleanup and led off the second. The Shitters' big hope was at the plate. The bench began to talk it up. The Mill Town fans also came alive and began demanding a rally. Donkey Nuts stepped in and scowled at Doolan. He was still scowling three pitches later as he walked back to the bench. He hadn't even swung the bat. He hadn't even seen the ball. The Mill Town crowd quietly settled back for a long afternoon. Gordie held the Big Bend crew to a couple of scrawny base hits and no score in the bottom of the second and watched his next three hitters go down in order in the top of the third.

He had two outs in the bottom of the third when Big Bend managed to drill a single between third and short. The next guy up hit a fly ball to short center that Donkey Nuts couldn't get to. By the time he came up with it Big Bend had men on first and third with two outs.

"C'mon Gordie, just one more, let's go, babe," yelled Danny from short. Gordie looked around and checked his outfield. Emery was playing deep in left for a right-handed hitter, Donk was in straightaway center field and By God Harry was deep in right field smoking a big fat cigar. He claimed it kept the mosquitos and bugs away. George motioned him in to short right field in case the hitter popped one that way and By God moved slowly in, his cigar sending up periodic puffs of smoke.

Gordie turned back to concentrate on the hitter. He got a strike past him on the inside of the plate and then threw a ball just inside. Gordie figured to cross him up and came back with a fast ball on the outside of the plate that the hitter got behind on and popped out into short right just about where Gordie had positioned By God Harry. Willard started back on it but saw it was a little too far out and dropped off to give By God Harry plenty of room.

By God had plenty of room all right. At the crack of the bat, By God had turned and when Willard looked up he was legging it for the right field fence as fast as his lumbering legs would take him. "No! no!, no!," Willard yelled, but By God was determined to pick this one right off the wall. He still had his back turned and was pounding for the fence when the ball dropped in about 30 feet behind Willard and about 200 feet short of By God. By the time Willard could retrieve the ball, two runs were across and the hitter was standing on third.

Gordie wanted to kill his behemoth right fielder. But when he looked out into right field it looked like By God was about to expire on his own. He was bent over convulsing violently, shudders rattling his big body. Then he straightened up and headed for Gordie's pickup. He got to the truck and clawed frantically around in the back. By the time Gordie reached him, he had hoisted a quart of beer and was draining it in one gulp.

Gordie asked the question for the entire crowd, "What the hell are you doing?"

"By God, nothin', I swallowed that friggin' cigar and it was still lit."

Gordie got out of the inning, but the Shitters were two runs down and, the way Doolan was pitching, did not have very bright prospects of getting them back. By God was his leadoff hitter so things looked dim indeed.

"Get up there you big fart and do something right," squeaked Sammy from his spot on the end of the bench.

A chagrined By God just looked at him and approached the plate. He had taken his coveralls off when he put on his game shirt and there was about a foot and a half of immense beer belly bulging out between the bottom of his shirt and the top of his pants. Right in the middle was a belly button the size of a small wading pool. By God dug in and squinted out at Doolan. Doolan fired one that popped in the catcher's mitt like a firecracker. The catcher was starting to throw it back when By God took a vicious cut level and true right across the middle of the plate. He was a little bit behind the pitch.

Doolan fired another one that got away from him entirely and sent the players on the Big Bend bench ducking for cover. By God took another wicked cut level and true right across the middle of the plate. Gordie could only bury his head in his glove.

Doolan was a little rattled by the wild pitch but was even more rattled by the fact that By God had swung at it. He lost his concentration momentarily and piped a screamer right over the middle of the plate.

By God took his regular cut and it was one of those rare moments in time when all other elements of the universe were in their proper places. The ball was at precisely the right height, precisely across the middle of the plate and By God swung at precisely the time the ball reached the plate and he got precisely the fat part of the bat on it with precisely all of his considerable weight behind it. The ball rocketed over the left center field fence before the outfielder could even turn around and watch it sail far and away out onto Route 11.

The Mill Town fans went out of their minds. They were on their feet screaming and pounding each other on the back. The Shitters were up and off the bench hugging each other. They had new life.

In all the tumult, it took Gordie a couple of minutes to realize that By God was still standing at the plate. He stood with the bat in his hand transfixed, staring at the spot where the ball had sailed over the outfield fence. He was stunned. His boozed-soaked mind could not absorb the fact that he had actually hit the ball.

"Run, By God, run!" Gordie yelled as he frantically began waving By God toward first. By God turned and looked at him but nothing was registering.

"You've got to run the bases! Run!" Gordie screamed.

The crowd picked it up. "Run, By God, run! Run, By God, run! Run By God run!" It came to By God that he had something of some urgency to do and he headed out for first. He did not take the homerun hitter's traditional jog around the bases. He put his head down and started running as fast as he could toward first. As fast as he could amounted to a plodding, almost slow motion gait, but By God felt like he was flying. He rounded first and headed toward second and he could feel his legs begin to tighten up. He eventually made a sweeping turn around second that took him halfway into left field and Gordie could see that he was in trouble.

"Slow down, By God, take it easy," Gordie yelled. By God could not have been going much slower, but he was putting everything he had into it. He was pounding down the baseline hoping he could make it to the plate before his aching legs seized up all together. He rounded third a desperate panic-stricken man. He could no longer control his legs. He was telling them to keep going, but they were deciding to go in two different directions at once – sideways. A bonfire had broken out in his lungs. He began to wobble, stagger, lurch and sag. Halfway to the plate, he pitched forward on his face. He was done.

Gordie raced down the third base line and stood over the exhausted log skidder. "Get up! Get up! Get up!" he screamed. "You've got to touch the plate!"

By God raised his head from the dust and looked pleadingly at Gordie. Gordie sympathetically began kicking him in the ass. "Get going you beer belching son of a bitch," he ranted. "I'll kill ya if ya don't get goin'!"

By this time the rest of the team was surrounding Gordie on the third base line urging the tortured man on. Sammy and Hung were down on their hands and knees begging By God to make it the last few feet.

By God reached down inside himself, deeper than he ever thought he could and got up on his elbows. His legs would have nothing to do with him so he began to pull himself forward with his arms, clawing at the dust for any handhold he could get. He began to inch forward and the crowd began to roar again. Even the Big Bend fans were cheering him on. It took forever and every inch was a victory over pain and nausea, but By God was finally able to reach out and touch the corner of the plate. It was two to one.

As By God lay there in the dirt waiting for a welcome death, he could hear the crowd roaring its admiration and he knew it was somehow for him, but he was too far gone to bring it into focus. All he knew is that he wanted to die and the sooner the better. He felt himself being lifted up and dreamily thought it must be the angels come to carry him home. But it was only the entire Shitters softball team getting him out of the way so they could continue the game.

Doolan was furious that he had let anyone get good wood on the ball. It was the first time in three leagues in four seasons that anyone had hit a homerun off him. He ended the inning by blowing three pitches each by Tink, Danny and Hung.

Big Bend managed to get a couple of guys on base in the bottom of the fourth, but some slick fielding by Hung and Danny put an end to their rally.

The dreaded fifth ining arrive, but the Shitters weren't able to turn it around. Some chinks did appear in Doolan's armor as Donkey Nuts slammed a line drive right into the first baseman's mitt and Gordie nailed one that took the right fielder all the way to the wall. But the fifth inning ended with Big Bend still up two to one and the umpires signaled a temporary halt to the action. Gilles and a couple of Big Bend players went to Gilles' station wagon and came back with their arms loaded with about every assortment of women's lingerie imaginable. They plopped the garments down on the bench in front of the Shitters. "Ok, girls, fix yourselves up real nice now," crowed Gilles.

"Screw you, you bastard," Gordie growled as he scooped up most of the clothes. "C'mon you guys, over by the trucks and let's get into this stuff and get it over with." The Shitters reluctantly followed him into the parking lot.

The fans stood up and stretched and some drifted off to the concession stand for hotdogs and soda while others went behind the bleachers to knock down a couple of cold beers. The contingents from both towns were carefully keeping their distance from each other even when ordering refreshments and they gathered in two different groups at opposite ends of the bleachers to discuss the details of the first five innings.

The Mill Town crowd was lamenting the half-game situation when one woman looked over her shoulder and said, "Oh, my God, would you look at that!" They all turned to see the Shitters slinking between cars in the parking lot as they headed back toward the field.

The Big Bend fans spotted them about the same time and the early evening air was filled with the peals of laughter. They were in stitches as they pointed from one player to another and convulsed in a new series of giggles and guffaws.

The Shitters were a sight. They had all stripped down to their jockey shorts and spikes. Donkey Nuts had put on a pair of white panties and a bra that contrasted sharply with the black hair that covered his entire gorilla form. Hung was wearing a powder blue chamois that was about four sizes too small for him and threatened to squeeze his oversized love muscle right up into his belly. He could barely walk.

Glenn Tink was wearing a nursing bra that dwarfed his sparrow chest and every time he moved the straps slipped off his shoulders and the bra dropped down to his waist. He also was wearing a garter belt that he managed to get attached to a pair of stockings that hung on his skinny legs like a pair of waders. Sammy had been the last to pick from the lingerie pile and was left with a pair of yellow bloomers of gargantuan proportions. He had grabbed two handfuls of the front of the drawers and was looking around for something to tie them up with when Gordie took hold of the tops and wrapped them all the way around Sammy's waist and tied a knot in front.

"I'd sure as hell hate to get caught under the fat ass whale that wears these things," Sammy said to no one in particular as he stood there looking like a diapered doll.

Gilles, who was chortling nearby, stopped laughing. He had spent half the morning talking his wife out of them.

But of all the ungodly sights on that field, by far the ungodliest was By God Harry who had managed to recover somewhat from his trip around the bases. By God was not in the habit of wearing underwear and when he saw all those frilly panties, he figured he had better go for something more substantial or he would be hanging out for all the world to see. So he grabbed a panty girdle that appeared to be made of sterner stuff. He had somehow managed to stretch it over his immense legs to the point where his private parts were covered, but he could not even come close to getting it started over his huge belly. Hung and Donkey Nuts had taken hold on either hip and had pulled up as hard as they could but to no avail. He waddled back to the bench with the girdle just above his pubic hairs in front and halfway up the crack of his ass in back. That was the best he could do and By God that was going to have to be it.

The rest of the Shitters were outfitted in a similar assortment of garments and they were getting ready for the top of the inning when Gordie suddenly had two of the best ideas he had ever come up with. He called his players around him and explained his strategy for the second half of the game.

"Ok, we've gotta get some runs, right? We've gotta be ahead of them by the bottom of the seventh if we're going to make them get into these fairy outfits. The only way we're goin' to do that is to get Doolan rattled. Well, I think I got a way, and he explained what he wanted them to do.

After briefing the players, he called Peg aside. "I think we can get to Doolan all right, but we need to keep them from scoring. I got an idea how to keep them offstride," and he explained it to Peg.

As Doolan approached the mound to start the sixth, Hung called to him in a falsetto voice, "Hey, sweetheart, wanna go out behind the barn and play?"

Gordie had made sure the details of Doolan's rejection from the Army had spread through the crowd and the stands erupted with laughter.

"Hey, Doolan, how about playing a tune on my pipe organ," called out Glenn Tink and the Mill Town fans roared again. Smoke began to curl up Doolan's ears and he fired a warmup pitch right over the backstop.

"My, you are so strong for a girl," called Gordie in a mincing voice and Doolan grew even hotter.

"Oh my goodness, oh my dear, Doolan's feeling kind of queer," sang Rhymin' Roy, and Doolan fired another one over the backstop.

"You finally made up one of those things that makes sense," Donkey Nuts said to Rhymin' Roy.

By now the Mill Town fans had joined in the harassment and they were giving Doolan fits. He could barely see straight and kicked savagely at the mound. He wanted to kill somebody but could do little more than squeeze the life out of the softball and wish he were dead.

Figuring that Doolan's control was in some jeopardy, Gordie sent Sammy in to pinch hit for Emery. Sammy would be about as small a target as Doolan would ever pitch to.

It was going to be a challenge to get the ball into Sammy's abbreviated strike zone as it was, but when Sammy stepped into the box in his wraparound bloomers, he stopped, tapped the dirt off his spikes and blew Doolan a big fat kiss.

Doolan went wild. He charged the plate winding up as he ran. He was going to take Sammy's head off. He was half way to the plate when he fired the ball as hard as he could. The Big Bend catcher jumped up to restrain him, Sammy flattened himself in the dirt and the umpire took the shot an inch and a half below his chest protector, right on the end of his fun and games. A big ex-coal miner, he hopped around the plate yipping like a puppy for about 30 seconds and then dropped to his knees holding himself as gently as he could.

It was bedlam on the field. Donkey Nuts and Danny were restraining a wild-eyed Doolan who was trying to get to Sammy who had run around and hid behind Peg. The players on both teams were squared off with each other waiting for someone to make the next move. The plate ump was on his knees in the dirt bent over like a holy man in prayer and was in no condition to take charge, so the ump on the bases came running in and declared that Doolan's action was unsportsman-like and ordered him out of the game.

Gilles protested as best he could, but the sight of the big man in black quivering in the dust at home plate took a lot out of his argument. Doolan made a beeline for his car and, without even taking his spikes off, roared out of the parking lot to look for a bar where he could drown out the taunts and laughter of the crowd.

It was about 10 minutes before the plate ump was able to get to his feet and gingerly return to his duties. By that time the crowd had settled back down and Gilles decided he would have to pitch the rest of the game himself. After their initial anger at Doolan being banished, the Big Bend fans returned to their giggling and tee-heeing at the ridiculous outfits on the Shitters. Their laugher quieted, however, when Gilles walked Sammy and he ended up on first looking like a yellow daffodil growing out of the base. Their concern deepened when Rhymin' Roy hit a shot to deep right center field that had extra bases written all over it. Sammy lit out for second as fast as his sawed off legs would carry him and in surprisingly short order he was around second and on his way to third. He was halfway to third when he realized something was slipping. The knot in his bloomers was coming undone! He grabbed the front of them with both hands just as they started to fall and came pounding around third with a yard of yellow rayon in each fist. He scored the tying run standing up and was surrounded by his teammates and the roar of the crowd.

Two pitches later Rhymin' Roy scored as Willard drilled a shot up the middle. Willard made the mistake of rounding first with his head down convinced that he had an easy double. By the time he looked up and saw the roving fielder standing on second with the ball it was too late to do anything but say "Oh shit" and run right into the tag.

Henry Wabash managed to pop a pinch hit back to Gilles for the second out and By God Harry waddled up to the plate. He could barely move in his corset, but it did give some support to his aching legs. He felt a little conspicuous with half of his ass sticking out for all the crowd to see, but he put that behind him as he prepared to blast another one out of the park. But this time the universal elements did not come together. Gilles' first pitch slipped out of his hand, hit the ground about three feet in front of the mound and rolled across the plate. By God swung so hard the panty girdle got twisted around on him and he had to have Gordie twist it back.

The next pitch from Gilles swooped up into the air and plopped in the dust about six feet short of the plate. This time By God's vicious cut sent him sprawling. He got up, dusted himself off and set himself for the next pitch. Gilles reached for his handkerchief in his hip pocket and By God, thinking it was the high hard one, swung for all he was worth. A puzzled Gilles dutifully lobbed the ball to the plate as By God was screwing himself into the ground. By God slowly disentangled himself and shuffled back to the bench muttering, "He pulled the string on me."

They went into the bottom of the sixth with the Shitters up 3 to 2 and the Big Bend crew was determined to get the runs back. Gordie took his warmup pitches as Peg went along the third base line coaxing cheers out of the Mill Town crowd. The first Big Bend hitter of the inning stepped into the box and faced Gordie. By the time Gordie fired the first pitch right down the middle, however, the ball was the last thing on the batter's mind. He was staring bug-eyed down the third base line where Peg was jumping up and down rooting for her boys. But Peg had stripped off her team shirt with the double zeroes and was cheering away in only her bra with the eighth and ninth wonders of the world bobbing up and down like a pair of huge water balloons. Gordie fired two more strikes that neither the hitter nor the plate umpire saw. Peg had lined herself up with the third base coach so that when the batter looked down to get the sign, he couldn't miss Peg's double-barreled assets. And to make it even harder for the batter, so to speak, as soon as he set himself she would begin jumping up and down, setting in motion one of the most fascinating violations of the law of gravity anyone on the field had ever seen.

Gilles was beside himself. "No way! No way!" he raged at the plate ump after his first batter had been called out on strikes. "They can't do that!"

Gordie walked in off the mound. "What are you talking about? Can't do what?" he asked innocently.

"You know god-damned well what," Gilles fumed. "You can't let her stand out there with her tits hanging out. It ain't right."

"What are you talking about?" said Gordie. "You're the one that said the team that is behind after five has to dress up in women's underwear. Well, she's on our team. Just 'cause she happens to be a woman is a coincidence."

"That's God-damned sneaky and you know it," said Gilles, but the plate umpire ruled in favor of the Shitters, partly because they were right and partly because he was not about to cover up the most stimulating works of art he had seen in years. It actually presented him with an erotic dilemma because he was still hurting from Doolan's assault on his water works. His pain increased in proportion to his appendage every time he looked at Peg, but it was a sweet ache.

The next two Big Bend hitters went down in order without complaint. In fact the umpire had to tap them on the shoulder to tell them when they had taken their third called strikes. They were too busy trying to pick up the sign.

The Shitters also went hitless in the top of the seventh due to some superior fielding on Big Bend's part. Big Bend came to the plate in the bottom of the seventh determined to avoid the humiliation of dressing in drag. But Peg was too much for them. She added a new twist, or more accurately, bow, to her cheerleading routine. Just as the hitter looked down to third, she would lean forward and put her hands on her knees just like the third base coach. Except that when she bent over those special attractions threatened to fall right out of her bra. And those hitters were not about to miss it if they did. The more that flesh strained to get loose, the more the hitters were mesmerized. It was no contest. Gordie had two strikeouts before Peg straightened up for the first time. The plate ump was also having a little trouble straightening up.

The only threat Big Bend made in the inning was when Gilles, who was madder than he was horny, hit a ground ball to Hung at third. Hung picked it up and rifled it to Willard on first. But Willard never saw it. What Willard saw when he looked to third for the throw were the objects of his affection swinging in the breeze like a couple of succulent pendulums. Willard took the softball right smack in the mouth and didn't even blink lest he lose a fraction of a second of this wondrous sight.

He later swore it was worth every one of the three broken teeth.

With the scoreboard at the end of the seventh reading three to two for the Shitters, the game was again stopped and another pile of undies was hauled out for the Big Bend players to reluctantly choose from.

They also retreated to the parking lot and stripped down to their shorts. They returned looking every bit as foolish as the Shitters in a colorful assortment of panties and bras, girdles and stockings and slips. Even Gilles had allowed himself to be tied into one of those wraparound girdles that lace in the back. It was now the Shitters turn to crack up and they did just that. The Mill Town fans also got their digs in as the lingerie -clad gladiators took the field for the top of the eighth.

As the game got under way again, 200 years of animosity began to dissolve. It started slowly with a Mill Town fan remarking to a Big Bend fan on how ridiculous both teams looked. And the Big Bend fan agreed! History in the making! Others began to exchange good-natured comments on this or that outfit they thought was particularly hilarious and soon there was bipartisan laughter running through the crowd. Now that both teams looked like refugees from the women's pages of a Sears catalog, there was no reason for resentment on either side. How can you stay mad when the object of your animosity is one of the funniest looking sights you have ever seen?

The thawing of the intra-town relations didn't reach the players right away. They continued to glower at each other as they fidgeted in their feminine garments. It wasn't until Glen Tink managed to make it to first on a slow roller down the third baseline that a new level of community rapport was reached. Tink was standing on first, a vision of loveliness in his nursing bra, garter belt and sagging stockings when one got away from Gilles and it went over the catcher's head. Tink took off for second and big Boonie Wilson, who was playing first for Big Bend in a shocking pink sheer negligee, panicked. He reached out and grabbed the rear straps of Tink's garter belt as he went by. The elastic stretched as far as it was about to beforeTink was brought to a halt. Tink kept trying as hard as he could to run, but Boonie outweighed him by close to 200 pounds and Tink wasn't getting anywhere as long as the elastic held.

The sight of Tink leaning toward second like a hapless soul bucking a strong wind and Booonie hauling back like a mule skinner trying to rein in a runaway team was too much for even the players.

The Shitters bench began to roar with laughter and the Big Bend players were rolling around on the ground in convulsions. Boonie and Tink were the only two people in the ballpark who were not cracking up. They continued their tug of war with riveted determination until it finally came to them that the whole world was laughing at them. Tink turned and looked back at Boonie whose negligee had slipped off one shoulder in their struggle.

"What are you trying to do, seduce me, you harlot?" he said and Boonie broke into a grin.

"By golly, you are kind of cute," he said and slipped his arm around Tink's waist and began dancing down the first base line with him. The place went wild. Players from both teams began mingling and commenting on each others outfits. The base ump came up with the idea of a lingerie fashion show and got the Big Bend team lined up at third and the Shitters lined up at first. At his signal, a player from each team would sashay to home plate. The players were into it now and began trying to outdo each other in showing off their apparel. They began bowing, turning, swirling and pirouetting down the baselines as they headed toward home. As they reached the plate, they paired off and promenaded arm in arm in front of the crowd. Someone in the crowd began singing A Pretty Girl is Like a Melody and everyone else joined in.

It was a grand moment in the antagonistic history of the two towns and was made even grander when Gilles, in a weak moment, declared that drinks were on the house for both teams. The Big Bend Grill was just across Route 11 from the ball park and the players, well aware of Gilles' legendary tightwadery, wasted no time getting across the road and into the bar. None of them bothered to take time to change and the place was soon filled with about 30 of the hairiest, ugliest creatures perched on barstools in panties, pantaloons, stockings, brassieres and negligees, swilling down beer.

While they were enjoying their brew, Rodney Towder was beginning to squirm. He had been driving for four hours and had had to piss for two, but his wife, Alma, had rejected every place he suggested they stop. She was a finicky woman who couldn't stand a restaurant that was the least bit dirty or untidy and would get up and walk out if she was displeased with anything. It made for difficult traveling for Rodney who had an undersized bladder and an oversized thirst. The only tolerable part about traveling with Alma were the frequent stops he was forced to make because of his urinary handicap. While Alma waited in the car, he would hurry into the establishment to use the men's room. It also gave him the opportunity to knock down a couple of shots or beers before hurrying back to the car.

Rodney's problem was that Alma had to approve the places he stopped at even when she didn't go in. "I'm not going to have you catching something in one of those restrooms and then passing it on to me," she would say. And so Rodney would keep suggesting places and she would keep turning them down until his teeth were floating and his hair felt like seaweed. After tiring of his anguished pleas, she would finally relent to his stopping at some reasonably respectable place.

Reasonably respectable had nothing to do with the Big Bend Grill, but by the time they were approaching it, Rodney was beyond worrying about respectability. He was worrying about flooding the front seat of his 1955 Cadillac. "For God's sake, Alma, I can't wait any longer. I'm in pain," he whined.

"All right, all right, go into that place with the polka dots on it, but make sure you go standing up. That place looks like it could have all kinds of things. I don't even know where we are." "We're in Pennsylvania somewhere near Scranton. We won't be in New Jersey for quite awhile," said Rodney as he scrambled from the car looking forward to a good piss and a couple of shots of whiskey.

Alma settled back in her seat for the usual long wait for Rodney to empty his bladder. She never could understand why it took him so long to go to the bathroom when they were traveling. It never took him that long at home. She was just beginning to close her eyes when Rodney came back out the front door, a look of panic on his face. I think he wet himself, she thought as he scurried to the car.

"What in the world happened? Didn't you make it in time?" she asked as he climbed into the car and started the engine.

"Never mind, you wouldn't believe it if I told you."

"Well, look at you, you're a sight. Didn't they have a bathroom?" Alma asked as Rodney sped away on Route 11.

"Alma, I'd rather ride all the way to Red Bank soaking wet than use that bathroom with a bar full of what I saw in there. Just be thankful that one of them didn't take a liking to me."

Alma gave him a puzzled look. "God, 58 years old and he's starting to lose it already."

WHAT ARE FRIENDS FOR?

"Excuse me, bartender, but I'm looking for someone to take me on a rattlesnake hunt."

Johnny had seen her get out of the car and had stopped loading coolers to drink in the sight as she approached the front door. She was the most striking woman he had seen in years and looked totally out of place in The Club. She appeared to be in her late 20s, was as tall as Johnny and carried herself with absolute assurance. Full, shoulder-length brown hair fell around a beautiful oval-shaped face. Her large brown eyes were accentuated by a crisp professional makeup job. Her full lips were carefully outlined with a wet, red lipstick. She wore a cinnamon-colored tweed blazer and skirt that hugged full, round hips and long tapered legs. Despite her height, she wore heels that not only added an inch but gave her a provocative carriage as she moved to the bar and made her inquiry.

Johnny and Starley Basil were the only people in The Club when she came in. It was mid-afternoon and the regulars still had a couple of hours of labor before paying their dues for the day.

"What is it you wanted?" Johnny wasn't sure he had heard her right.

"The first thing I would like is a nice, cold beer," she said as she slid easily onto a bar stool. She couldn't be more comfortable, Johnny thought, despite the fact she obviously didn't belong in a small town saloon. She had career woman written all over her and there weren't all that many career women walking into bars in Mill Town or anywhere else in the 1950s.

"The beer I can take care of," Johnny said. "Now what was the rest of it?" He drew a draft and set it in front of her.

"This is a nice little place. What is is called?"

"I never really got around to naming it, I guess. Some of the young guns call it The Club, but that's just their own little joke. You can see it's no club. Most people just call it Johnny's. That's me."

"Oh, you're the owner?" she said, a bit surprised. "Well, maybe you can help me. My name is Beth Barrett. I'm a reporter for the Binghamton Press. One of my editors heard that people down here go rattlesnake hunting and we thought it might make a good feature story."

"You want to write about rattlesnakes?"

"What I would really like to do is to be able to go out for a day with somebody so I can see just how they do it and to get some pictures. Do you think that would be possible?"

"Oh, it's possible all right. But I'm damned if I know why you would want to tromp around the woods looking for rattlesnakes. Seems like there are a lot of better things to write about."

"You don't think rattlesnake hunting is something unusual to write about?"

"It's not for me, but I grew up with them on the farm. They're a real pain because you got to keep watching out for them when you're out in the fields."

"Then you do have them around here?"

"Oh, we've got them all right. But you don't find them all over. Most of them seem to be along the ridge between here and Big Bend. It's rocky land and they seem to like that. You find one once in awhile scattered around other places but most of them are along that ridge. I know our place was loaded with them. You go out to get the cows and you really had to watch where you were going."

"What do you do when you find them?"

"What do you do? You kill them deader than hell. Who wants a live rattlesnake?"

"I thought you got venom or something out of them for medicine."

"You mean milking them? They do that farther down state. They get whole bunches of people going out and catching them alive and selling them. We don't do that. We just try to clean them out so the kids don't get hurt. And some of the farmers think the rattlers bite their cows and make them sick, but I don't hold with that."

"Is it true the meat is a real delicacy?"

"Lady, what is it, Beth? You're asking the wrong man. I wouldn't anymore eat rattlesnake meat than I would a skunk. I don't know anyone around here who eats the meat. About all they do around here is skin 'em out and nail the skin and rattles on the side of the barn. Everybody likes to brag about how big the snake was or how many rattles it had, but that's about it."

"It sounds to me like it still might make an interesting story. I must admit

I'm not too wild about snakes, but I grew up on a farm so I'm not a complete stranger to them. My daddy used to kill them once in awhile. They weren't poisonous, though."

"You grew up on a farm?" Johnny couldn't believe he was looking at a farm girl, not with the tailored outfit and the worldly assurance.

Beth explained that she was from Missouri where her father had a 400-acre farm a few miles from Independence. He was not an especially competent farmer and, for all his hard work, barely squeezed a living out of the land, so the family was always struggling. Her mother made all of the clothes for Beth and her sister, Teddy, when they were in school and she wasn't anymore competent a seamstress than her husband was a farmer. The girls grew up knowing they looked different in their poorly made outfits and hating every stitch. Kids in grade school, especially the town kids, gave them a rough time and they spent many lonely school bus rides home in tears.

Things began to change in junior high as they filled out and their features began to show promises of things to come. They both got jobs doing housecleaning after school and saved every nickel for clothes. They had no TV and spent isolated hours on their farm pouring through catalogs discussing styles and fashions and deciding what particular things would look best on them. When they would get enough money they would get their father to drive them in to Independence where they would spend the day looking for just the right clothes at just the right prices. They were just a year apart and could swap clothes with no problem so each had a keen interest in what the other was buying.

By the time they reached high school, the young studs really began to take notice. At first, the girls thought it was their new wardrobes, but it didn't take long for them to find out it was something else. Beth rounded out quite early and had seniors chasing her when she was a sophomore. She delighted in the attention and could act as silly as any 14-year-old, but young as she was, she still had control of her situation. Those painful childhood years had left her with a feeling of being different despite being the prettiest girl in her class. She didn't want to take a chance on more pain so she was careful about committing her feelings more than she thought was safe. She was outgoing, generous and willing to do anything for anybody but did not open the door all the way. She had a couple of relationships with boys who she found fun and comfortable, but nothing that she couldn't walk away from. Her senior year was filled with parties, dances and backseat cuddling and she was looking forward to graduation and a good-paying job.

It was in the spring of her senior year that her father collapsed and died while plowing. Beth felt sad about his death, but she felt sadder about his life and the fact he had left it after all those years of struggle and near-failure where he seemed to have so little control over his destiny. She vowed it would not be her fate. Her mother also vowed her daughters would not face a lifetime of not caring whether the morning came ever again. They would not face the sameness that comes from hopelessness.

Her husband was barely in the ground before she was arranging to sell off several acres closest to town. She was sending her daughters to college and a better life. Beth had always been strong in English. She also had always wanted to travel and often imagined herself a correspondent traveling all over the world. So she attended the University of Missouri and majored in journalism. She adapted quickly and happily to college life, finding it exciting to be mixing with a more urbane and intellectual element than she had found at home. She also felt, although a bit guilty, a welcome relief to turn her back on her farm girl existence. She had no desire to go back to her roots. She was determined to see the world and the first step on that journey was a job as a general assignment reporter on the Binghamton Press. She had grown more comfortable casually mentioning her rural background and it was this piece of information that got her the assignment of hunting rattlesnakes.

"So, what do you think? Is there someone who could take me on a hunt?" she asked Johnny after they had talked awhile about snakes and farms and small towns. "I stopped in your drugstore and they told me that, if I wanted to find rattlesnake hunters, this would be the place to look."

"Well, it's the right place all right, and almost the right time. They all come piling in here soon as the freezer plant lets out and the sawmill whistle blows. There are bound to be some rattlesnake hunters among them." Johnny couldn't wait to see the expressions on the faces when those yahoos saw what was waiting for them. There hadn't been a woman this classy looking in town since Governor George Leader had brought his wife through on a campaign tour four years earlier.

They had almost an hour to kill and Johnny was surprised at how well Beth could handle her beer. She was not one to coast and the two of them downed several as they chatted. He also was surprised at how easy she was to like. She was sophistication personified, but was also one of the most unassuming people he had ever met. She was good company. All too soon for Johnny, the blast of the sawmill whistle across the street set every dog in town howling and sent its shrill message that it was time for that wonderful hour or so between the problems at work and the problems at home. The whistle was for the sawmill crew, but the message was for anyone in town who needed it.

Within a few minutes they began trooping in the front door and they brought the smell of pine, maple, oak, cedar and sweat with them. They piled through the door a jumble of conversation that petered out to silence as they became aware of Beth. There clearly was a foreigner in their midst, a beautiful intimidating foreigner and they were uneasy about it. They drew together at one corner of the bar and began murmuring to each other while Beth sat relaxed and amused with Johnny standing across the bar from her even more amused.

"What's the matter with you clowns? Haven't you ever seen a reporter before?" Johnny said. "This is Beth Barrett from the Binghamton Press and she is looking for someone to take her on a rattlesnake hunt."

That made even less sense to them and they continued to stare.

"Well, come on, you guys drinkin' or not?" Johnny finally asked. "Let me buy a round, Johnny, these gentlemen look like they have put in a hard day," Beth offered.

"Fine with me," said Johnny and he began to set them up. Beer on the bar got most of them feeling more at home and they nodded their thanks to Beth as they lifted their glasses. "To ya," said Petey Slater as he saluted her with his glass before draining it in one gulp. Free beers didn't come often to Petey and he wasn't about to let it get away.

Conversation returned to a more normal level as they drank, but they kept stealing glances at Beth. She was clearly out of their league, but that didn't keep them from wanting to look. The bar began filling up as others in town responded to the whistle and Beth was soon flanked by men who wanted to talk but who didn't know what to say. They had no way of knowing that many of them reminded her of her father and the daily struggle to get by that he had shared with them. Her empathy slowly began to reach them as she chatted with first one and then another and, as the afternoon deepened, she had made a friend of just about everyone in the bar. And one worshiper.

Sammy Griney was more than smitten. He was mesmerized. Johnny had introduced him and Beth had offered her hand and a smile. Women didn't shake hands with men back then and Sammy didn't know what to do. But there that pretty little hand was in front of him and he didn't know what to do except to take it as gently as he could in his own little hand. She didn't seem to mind the mill grime he hadn't taken the time to wash off. She asked Sammy what he did at the mill and appeared impressed when he told her he operated the big saw, the one with the blade taller than he was, and how he could slice a three-foot-thick log into one-inch boards in a matter of minutes. He didn't tell her that the whole operation was done mechanically and that all he had to do was to keep an eye on it to keep the saw from binding. It sounded more important the way he told it. If there was anything that Sammy wanted to be at that moment was more important and a helluva lot taller. He found himself balancing on one leg on the foot rail in an effort to add a couple of inches and it brought him eye to eye with the seated object of his adoration, but it also put a severe cramp in the instep of his foot. The pain in his foot and the strain of balancing on one leg caused him to wince and tremble like someone on the immediate edge of a convulsion, but he hung on as long as he could hold Beth's attention.

"What the hell's the matter with you, Sammy? You look like you're about to take a fit," said Donkey Nuts as he stepped up to be introduced. As soon as he had come in the front door he had been told about Beth and he had made his way down the bar to see for himself. He was not one to introduce himself so he waited for Sammy to do it. Sammy had no intention of sharing his introduction time no matter how painful it was becoming so he ignored Donkey Nuts' remark.

"Why you perched up there like a one-legged rooster?" Donk wanted to know, although he had a very good idea why. Donk was not the kindest guy in the world. Sammy gave up and eased his quivering leg off the rail and resigned himself to the facts of life.

"This here is Donkey Nuts," he told Beth.

"Donkey Nuts?" she said.

"That's what they call me. Name's really Maynard."

That revelation drew its own murmur from the bar. Only a few of the regulars knew his real name.

Beth looked him over with interest. The physique was certainly impressive and would give any normal woman some warm thoughts, but his face was too full and his eyes too small to generate the warmth she liked to see in a man. She also could see that Donkey Nuts was not a sensitive soul and had a bit of a mean streak in him. A good part of his fun came at the expense of others. It wasn't something he did intentionally, It was just his nature.

"Well, Mr. Donkey Nuts, or Maynard, I'm told you do a lot of rattlesnake hunting."

"I go out once in awhile. Me and some of the other guys like to keep them cleaned out."

"Did they tell you I would like to do a story about it?"

"Yeah, they said you wanted to go with us. But I don't know. It don't seem like somethin' that women oughta be doin'."

"I'm not afraid of snakes if that's what you mean. I grew up on a farm so I'm not a stranger to them. You wouldn't have to worry about me."

"Maybe not, but you never know how someone's goin' to act when they come on their first rattler. Some people'd like to shit their pants."

Sammy winced at the language, but Beth let it roll right by.

"I'll tell you what. My paper will spring for a couple of cases of beer and you can have any of the pictures that are left over," said Beth.

Donkey Nuts got interested. The beer and the thought of following around behind her in the woods erased his reservations about women on a rattlesnake hunt.

"Ok, how about Saturday? We can meet up at my place and head out from there. I'll get a couple of the boys who know what they're doin' and we should have some luck. You best wear some boots and some long pants if you got them. The thicker the better."

"I have everything I need. I do some hiking when I get the chance."

"Ok, it's done then. Saturday morning eight o'clock sharp at my place," said Donkey Nuts and he got a pencil and paper from Johnny to write down directions for her.

"What kind of beer do you like?" she asked.

"Stegmaiers will do just fine. Long as it's cold," he said.

Beth stayed for a while longer until Sammy's stares got a bit awkward. She promised Johnny she would be sure to come back for another visit and made her exit under the gaze of every pair of eyes in the place.

As soon as she was out the door, the remarks began.

"Did you ever see such a butt in your life?" asked Willard Klemp. "You could have set a tea cup up on that ass it stuck out so far."

"It's the legs that got me," said Glenn Tink. "I ain't never seen a straighter pair of legs."

"Well, I was partial to the dairy section. There was just about enough there for me," said Shake Ketter.

"Why have you guys always got to drag it down in the gutter?" complained Sammy who was feeling insulted for Beth. "Somebody real nice like that and you got to start talkin' dirty." Donkey Nuts snorted. "We didn't say she wasn't nice. We just said she was built like a brick shithouse. What's the matter, you her boyfriend or somethin'?"

That drew a laugh all around and Sammy's sunburned face turned even redder. "No, I'm not, but you got no call to talk about her like that."

Sammy's right," said Johnny, who had his own feelings about Beth. "She's a class act and you ought to treat her that way. She seems to me to be about as nice as they come."

"Well, who the hell says she isn't?" Donkey Nuts was getting irritated. "She can be nice and sexy at the same time can't she? What the hell's wrong with that? My God, you guys are touchy." He couldn't understand what the big problem was but decided to change the subject anyway. He didn't like to see Johnny out of sorts.

"Ok, who wants to go Saturday? Clevis, how about you?" "Why, I suppose that might be a good thing to do. I suppose it might," said Clevis Randle who had done about as much rattlesnake hunting as anyone in The Club except

Donkey Nuts. "I wouldn't mind going. I haven't been out for awhile," said Clancy Rierdon.

"I been meanin' to get one to make a belt. The last one I got wouldn't even go around my waist," Gordie Alley said. "Besides, she might just decide to drag me off into the woods somewhere and I wouldn't not want to be there for that."

"Gordie, you got more shit than a cow drop," said By God Harry Hollis. "She'd rather cuddle up to a six-button diamondback than get next to you."

Sammy squealed. He was delighted to see Gordie get zinged. It didn't happen very often.

"What are you laughin' at you little piss pot?" said Gordie good naturedly. "She wouldn't even look at you. Even if she would, she couldn't see down that far."

Another round of laughter at Sammy's expense, but it didn't bother him. He was used to it and at least Gordie had been nailed once.

"Laugh all you want to. We'll see Saturday who she's nicest to," Sammy said.

That stopped everything. It was common knowledge at The Club that Sammy was terrified of snakes. Many a cruel joke had been played on him because of it. If things got too quiet in The Club, a sure fire way to stir things up was to pinch Sammy on the ankle and holler snake! It would send him straight up in the air and running around the room in a panic. No matter how many times it was pulled on him, it always worked.

Gordie Alley had once killed a harmless water snake and had thrown it in the back of his truck. When he got to The Club he had laid it on the front seat of Sammy's car. It was dark before Sammy had left The Club and as soon as he was out the front door, everyone hurried to the window to see what would happen. He started up the car and reached over on the seat for some cigarettes. What he got was a handful of snake. The terrified little man, screamed, threw his hands in the air and in his panic put the gas to the floor as his foot slipped off the clutch. His 1952 Pontiac rocketed forward and plowed head-on into the 200-year-old elm in the middle of the library lawn. The tree began to brown and died a few months later and the joke around The Club was that Sammy had scared it to death.

The most painful snake joke played on him happened at the sawmill and the pain was not all Sammy's. The noon whistle had blown and the crew had sat down in a big circle as usual to enjoy their lunch. Sammy had hauled out his big metal lunch pail ready for his usual three-sandwich feast unaware that someone had sabotaged it with a menacing-looking rubber snake. Sammy opened the pail to find a red-eyed monster staring at him.

He flew to his feet completely out of control. His right hand was still looped through the handle on the top of the lunch pail and he couldn't shake it loose. So he began swinging it around as hard as he could, anything to keep it away from him. The first thing he did was cold-cock Petey Slater with a round house shot behind his left ear. Petey pitched forward into the sawdust as the other men began ducking every which way to avoid the missile whirling wildly on the end of Sammy's arm. Sammy was berserk. He was oblivious to anyone around him. All he knew is that he had to kill that thing and he began beating the lunch pail against everything he could reach which just happened to be half of the sawmill crew.

Those who couldn't get out of range fell to the ground with their hands over their heads as Sammy beat on them with the lunch pail the way you would beat a rug. He was in the process of tenderizing some of the toughest backs in town when a couple of the guys who had escaped his attack sneaked up behind him and overpowered him. They had a tough time holding him down until one of them managed to get the lunch pail off his hand and out of his sight. He began to settle down as the men scattered around him painfully got to their feet. They lifted a groggy Petey Sater up and sat him on a stack of pallets where he started blowing sawdust out of his mouth and nose.

"Good God, man. I didn't know you were that scared of snakes," said Shake Ketter as he picked remnants of an egg salad sandwich out of his hair.

"I'm not afraid of them. I just don't like them," had been Sammy's reply.

And now he was declaring himself a member of the rattlesnake hunting party. "Now, Goddamn it, Sam, I'm not going out there in those woods with you jumpin' three feet in the air every time you see a crooked stick," Donkey Nuts said. "And I don't want to have to drag you off that hill if you drop over with a heart attack."

"I ain't goin' to have no heart attack and I ain't goin' to be jumpin' up in the air. I'm OK as long as you don't pull no friggin' surprises on me."

"Sammy, you know you faint at the picture of a snake. Who you tryin' to shit?" said Gordie. "You're just trying to impress that reporter."

"That ain't so, that just ain't so," Sammy protested, knowing full well that everyone knew Gordie was exactly right. But, despite the fact that she was way out of his short reach, he was determined not to miss out on a chance to see her again. And what if something happened where she had to be rescued and what if he were the only one around at the time and what if he did manage to save her from he wasn't sure what. Maybe then she wouldn't care how short he was or that he didn't have any teeth. Maybe, if he was a hero, those things wouldn't matter. He was determined not to miss out on his long shot opportunity and after a prolonged wrangle the rest of them could see they weren't going to be able to talk him out of it.

"Ok, you can go, but you're on your own. I don't want to hear no whinin' about you can't keep up," Donkey Nuts said.

"Don't worry about me. I've been in the woods plenty."

"I reckon that's true," said Gordie. "Everybody says you've been out in left field most of your life."

The following Saturday morning turned out to be a near perfect autumn day for snake hunting. It was a clear, crisp morning with a promise of warming up as the sun got into the sky. It was the kind of day that brought the snakes out on the rocks to sun themselves.

Beth had no problem finding Donkey Nuts' place despite the fact it was on a gravel road four miles back into the hills. She arrived in a pair of snug cream-colored cordoroy slacks, a red plaid flannel shirt under a water repellent brown jacket and a pair of hiking boots that came half way up her shapely calves. An expensive Roloflex camera hung from a strap around her neck. There was no question about it. Beth would look sexy wearing a Boy Scout tent. She made that hunting outfit look like a Dior fashion. And as she stood there in that hillside driveway, a lone female surrounded by men, it filled the air with a carnal feeling that didn't escape any of them.

"It certainly is beautiful out here," Beth said, looking out across the skyline of rolling hills. "We didn't have these kinds of hills back home. Everything was pretty much flat."

"Not everything was flat," Gordie whispered to Clancy as they left the porch and moved over to where Beth leaned against the trunk of her car.

"Are we about ready to start? Is it a good day for snakes do you think?" she asked.

"Everybody's here but Sammy," Donkey Nuts replied. "I'd just as soon take off without him. He won't be nothin' but a bother."

"Oh, I wouldn't do that. Not if he's counting on going. I put a bunch of beer in the cooler. Do you think it is too early to have one while we wait for him?" asked Beth.

Clevis smiled. "There's one thing my father taught me early on, God rest his soul, it's never too early for an eye opener and never too late for a night cap."

"He sounds like a wise old philosopher," Beth said smiling.

"Well, it turns out he wasn't all that wise and he didn't get all that old. His liver gave out on him when he was 46. But he surely did enjoy those 46 and that's what counts, isn't it?"

"I guess there's something to be said for that," Beth said, not quite sure what else to say, as she opened the trunk and passed the beers around.

The men were impressed as Beth drank straight from the can and stayed right with them as they went through two rounds and started on a third before Sammy's bucket of bolts came flying up the road throwing gravel every which way. He swung off the driveway and skidded to a halt, making Firestone gouges in a lawn that Donkey Nuts had only recently reseeded.

"God damn, Sam, what are you trying to do? I could plant potatoes in those tracks. My old lady is really goin' to be pissed," Donkey Nuts complained as a flustered Sammy jumped from his car.

"I'm sorry, Donk, I really am, but I was afraid I was goin' to miss you guys. I was afraid you was goin' to take off without me. I'd of been on time but this damned old gut bucket just died on me when I stopped for Homer Seer's cows and he had to go get his tractor and push me up Heart Lake hill so I could get a runnin' start down the other side and then Howard Bremmer's cows was crossin' and I had to stop for them and he had to give me a push and …"

"All right, all right, forget it," said Donkey Nuts impatiently, Let's just get started." He handed each of them, including Beth, a stick about five-feet long. They were all more or less about an inch thick and more or less straight and each had a Y at one end that could be used to pin a snake to the ground long enough to club it to death. He had a couple of burlap bags and he handed one to Clevis.

"What is this for?" Clevis asked.

"I just thought she might want to bring a snake or two back if we get any and we'd need something to carry them in," Donkey Nuts said.

"Well, I don't want to waste a good bag like this on a snake, but I can put it to good use if the young lady don't mind," said Clevis as he eyed the cooler. "Sure, help yourself, it's your beer," said Beth. "It might just hit the spot a little later on. We can use it to toast our victory."

Clevis loaded about a half a case of cans into the sack and slung it over his shoulder.

"We'll head back up behind the barn and check that ridge over toward East Lake," said Donkey Nuts. "It catches the sun early and we can nose around through Foster's quarry. Should be somethin' in there."

They rounded the barn with Donkey Nuts in the lead and Sammy bringing up the rear. Gordie stopped and ducked his head to light a cigarette and Sammy passed him. Gordie looked up to see Sammy hurrying along as best he could with a peculiar stiff-legged gait. He also saw that his sawed off lower legs were about twice as big around as they should be. His blue jeans bloused out at the knees and it was obvious there was more than Sammy under them. "He's walking like he's on stilts," Gordie thought to himself and he realized how ridiculous that idea was. Sammy was barely taller than the hay.

He watched Sammy stiff leg his way along for a few more yards before he said, "Sammy, what the hell are you up to?"

Sammy stopped. "What do you mean?"

"Why are you walkin' like you've got a carrot up your ass? And how come your pant legs are all bulged out?"

"I ain't doin' nothin'. Can't a guy walk without you jumping all over him? I got blisters, OK? Can't a guy have blisters for God's sake? What's the big deal?"

"You haven't got blisters. You weren't doin' that yesterday. What have you got under there?" and Gordie tapped his snake stick against Sammy's leg. He felt something solid and heard a metalic clink. "What the hell …" he said and tapped Sammy's shin again. Another clink.

"You got somethin' under there."

"No I haven't."

Clink.

"The hell you say."

Clink.

"I do not."

Clink.

"You do too."

Clink.

"Just get out of here."

Clink.

"By God, Sammy, you're trussed up in something," and Gordie hauled off and gave him a shot across both legs with his stick. Whack. It was solid as the side of a bar. Sammy never flinched. He barely felt it. Gordie used the Y of his stick and snagged the bottom of Sammy's pant leg and hoisted it up as far as he could and spotted bright silver metal.

"What the hell…?" and he quickly pulled up Sammy's pant leg to reveal a roll of roofing tin wrapped around his leg and tied with three strands of baling wire.

Gordie was about to call out to the others who had moved on ahead when Sammy pleaded in his little boy voice. "Don't say nothin', Gordie. I don't want them to know about it. I just couldn't go in them woods without somethin'. I can't stand the idea of gettin' bit by a snake."

Gordie was as fond of Sammy as anyone else in The Club despite all the fun he made of him and he realized how desperate he was to at least have a chance to make an impression on Beth. He knew that Sammy also realized how desperate and ludicrous an idea it was that he would even stand a chance with her. Gordie thought of how sad it was that the little man had to try to at least get close to her despite the certainty that she would never have any interest in him.

"I won't say anything, but it isn't going to make any difference. As soon as they see you walkin' like a ruptured duck, they're going to know there is something goofy going on. Look at the way your pants stick out."

"I know it, but I couldn't get it wrapped any tighter. I couldn't hold it and tie it at the same time."

"Well, c'mon, I'll try to help you," and Gordie rolled Sammy's pant leg up to his knee. He winced when he saw the back of his knee rubbed raw by the sharp edge of the tin. "God, Sammy, you're going to cut your damn legs off with these things."

"I know it. I made 'em too long. I can't hardly bend my knees without 'em diggin' right into me."

Gordie took out his handkerchief and ripped it in half. "It's too late to shorten them, but I can try and put some padding on them, maybe keep them from cuttin' into ya." He untied the wires and unwrapped the tin on Sammy's right leg. He rewrapped it and had Sammy hold it while he tied it tighter with half the handkerchief as padding behind his knee. He did the same with the left one. It took most of the bulge out of the pant legs and, if Sammy had been able to bend his knees, it would have been difficult to notice anything unusual. As it was, he still could barely bend his knees although it didn't hurt nearly as much. "Thanks, Gordie, for not sayin' nothin'. I don't need those guys makin' fun of me."

"I'm not going to say anything, but I still think you're nuts. You know it aint' goin' to get you anywhere."

"Yeah, I know it, but I wanted to come along anyway."

"We better get movin' then. They're going to be wonderin' where the hell we are." They set out through the field with Sammy hurrying along like a man with two wooden legs. They reached the wood line at the edge of Foster's quarry and found the rest of the party waiting for them. They were having another beer.

"What the hell happened to you guys?" Donkey Nuts asked. "Sam popped a couple of blisters and we were fixin' them up," Gordie said.

"Oh, are you OK, Sammy?" Beth asked, Can you walk on them?"

"Yeah, it ain't nothin'. I just have to walk kind of careful." He had a feeling he could tell her the truth about the whole thing and she would understand, but he didn't.

Beth lined them all up along a stone fence and took several shots of them as they stood awkwardly trying to look casual. Then Donkey Nuts outlined the plan of attack. Sammy, Gordie and Clancy would scout the lower edge of the quarry while he, Beth and Clevis headed up and checked the rim. They would meet at an outcropping of flagstone at the far end of the quarry. "Just what is the procedure if you find a snake? It might be a good thing for me to know," said Beth.

"You best give one of us a holler," Donkey Nuts said. "But, what you do is keep your distance and you just reach out real slow until you can pin him right behind the head with the end of your stick. You just hold him real tight 'til one of us can club the hell out of him."

"What if he decides to come after me?"

"He won't bother you unless you practically step right on him. He don't want no part of you and he will take off like a bat out of hell if he gets the chance. That's why you have to almost find them out sunnin' themselves to get a shot at them. You can find them under flat rocks, too, but you got to be real careful about liftin' the rocks."

"I think I'll just concentrate on the sunbathers," Beth said. Sammy was gulping down fear during Donkey Nuts instant lesson on snake snaring and he was already scanning every inch of ground around him as they prepared to make their way down to the base of the quarry.

Donkey Nuts, Beth and Clevis started up a long, steep path when Donkey Nuts stopped. "You go ahead, Clevis, I got to tie these rawhides," he said. Clevis and Beth continued up the path with Clevis in the lead. Donkey Nuts quickly fell in behind them and in a minute or two was enjoying the view he had been thinking about for three days. Beth's cheeks tightened under the light-colored cordoroys as she strained to climb the steep path and it served to make more pronounced the almost perfect roundness of her ass. The material stretched across her buttocks as she moved and climbed up into her crotch before traveling down her long, well-muscled legs. Donkey Nuts was no more than three feet behind her and feeling hornier by the minute. He had an incredible urge to reach out and kiss her right on the ass. "If she ever sat on a snake, by God, I'd be the first one right there to suck the poison out," he told himself as he watched her fluid motion making its way up the hill.

They reached the rim of the quarry and began making their way along the rock formation. It was late morning now and the sun had been warming the rocks for a couple of hours. Clevis had walked carefully out onto a rock shelf that overlooked the base of the quarry and the valley below and he turned and motioned for Beth and Donkey Nuts to stop. He slowly set down the bag of beer and began to push his snake stick out in front of him. He suddenly plunged the stick into the moss covering on the rock and leaned into it.

"By golly, I got him! And he ain't too happy about it!" Before Beth could see the snake, she could hear its rattle buzzing angrily. She had the presence to use her camera as Donkey Nuts stepped forward, pulling a long hunting knife out of a sheath on his belt.

"You got a good hold on him, Clevis?"

"Yessir, he's between a rock and a hard place now."

Donkey Nuts dropped to one knee beside Clevis and cut through the snake just behind Clevis' stick. The body continued to thrash around every which way for a few seconds and then it quieted down to slow rolls before it stopped all together. "He's not bad, he's got four buttons. Must be close to three feet long," Donkey Nuts said as he picked up the snake and showed it to Clevis.

"Hold it up so I can get a picture of you two with it," Beth said. Here, Clevis, it's your snake, you hold it, Donkey Nuts said. Clevis took the snake from him and held it up at arms length. He and Donkey Nuts stood stiff and straight as Beth took a couple of shots. Then Donkey Nuts cut the buttons off for a souvenir for Clevis and flung what was left out over the ledge into the valley. "Damn," he said almost as soon as he let it go, "I forgot Gordie wanted one for a belt, That one would have been long enough, too."

"It wouldn't have been a bad one," Clevis agreed. "But we ought to find some more. It's a good day for them." They continued to search the ridge, moving carefully across the moss-covered slabs of rock at the top of the quarry. They could look out and see across the valley the beautiful rolling hills that made Susquehanna County so special. They looked like a plate full of dumplings that someone had decorated with splashes of green, gold, brown and red. Each of them had two or three miniature barns, houses and silos carefully laid out.

"This is absolutely gorgeous," said Beth as she snapped some shots of the panorama before them. "At home it's as flat as a pancake compared to this."

"There ain't many places can match it," Clevis agreed. From the time he had been old enough to get up at 4 o'clock in the morning and do chores he had marveled at the way the sun rose over these hills and slowly brought up the colors and shapes hidden by the night. In the early mornings everything glistened wet and shiny and clean. It was one of the thing that kept Clevis at it all these years despite the fact he could barely make a living working the land and had always had to have another job to make ends meet. And it was one of the reasons Donkey Nuts stayed up on the hill rather than conveniently living in town where he could have walked to the feed mill where he worked. They made several more passes along the ridge and circled back through some rock formations a little lower, working their way down to the base of the quarry. Although he kept his eyes peeled for snakes, Donkey Nuts still got in a fair share of ass-viewing as he followed Beth across the terrain. He didn't know what he enjoyed more, the sloping mounds out across the valley or the pair three feet in front of him. Either way, he figured, he came out a winner.

Down below, Clancy, Gordie and Sammy worked the wide flagstone platform that formed the base of the quarry. It had been stripped and cleared to allow trucks to get in and stone masons had stacked carefully cut slabs that waited to be loaded. The three men checked these piles of soon-to-be-sidewalks cautiously. Sammy made sure he never got out in front as they approached a likely spot. He didn't hang back so much that it would be obvious, but he made sure he didn't get there first. Clancy had noticed Sammy's stilted stride as soon as they had started down the hill and had asked Gordie about it. Gordie knew Clancy was too soft-hearted to give Sammy a bad time so he told him what he had done and why he had done it.

"That poor little jerk. His legs must be killing him," Clancy said. "And he has to know it won't do him no good. It took a lot of guts for him to come out here looking for snakes when you're as scared of them as he is."

"I know it," said Gordie. "It just shows you what a woman can get you to do. Whatever you do, don't let Donkey Nuts know about it. He'd never let up on the poor little bastard."

"Naw, I wouldn't do that, but he's bound to see how goofy Sammy's walking."

"Maybe not, unless I miss my guess, he may be too busy lookin' at Beth to worry about Sammy."

They had been working the quarry for about a half hour when Clancy suddenly jammed his stick under a four-foot slab of rock that was tilted up on an angle. "Hey, hey, I got one!" he said in a voice about as loud as he would ever be likely to use. Sammy had been right behind Clancy and he yipped and jumped back about three feet at Clancy's sudden movement.

"Oh, my God, it's alive!" he squealed as he saw the snake's tail thrashing out from under the rock. Clancy kept a firm hold and Gordie found a solid piece of wood he could use for a club. "You're goin' to have to ease him out from under there so I can get a shot at his head," he told Clancy, who kept the pressure on, but began to carefully drag the snake out from under the rock. When Sammy saw the angry reptile, mouth wide open and hissing and trying to strike anything it could, he about lost it. His immediate fears eased, however, as Gordie began pulverizing the snake's head. In a matter of minutes Gordie was holding up a six-button diamond back no less than four feet long.

"Clancy, I think you just snagged me a No. 1 belt, unless you want him for yourself."

"Naw, he's all yours. I don't want nothin' to do with him."

"Well, maybe Sam wants to cut him up and cook him. You can have the meat, Sam, all I want is the skin."

Sammy almost got sick. He was still trembling just from seeing the snake and the thought of biting into it had his stomach rolling. "Goddamn it, Gordie, don't even say that. How can you even talk about eating it. My God, that's sick."

"Lots of people do," Gordie said, as he stretched the snake out on a flat rock and began slicing it along the belly. He skinned the snake out and cut off the buttons which he put in his pocket. He carefully rolled the skin up and put it in the burlap bag he was carrying. He took the carcass over to the edge of the rocks and threw it into the woods.

"It's your turn to find the next one," he told Sammy who had taken the opportunity to gently rub the backs of his tortured knees while Gordie was skinning the snake.

"Like hell," said Sammy, who already was feeling miserable about the way the day was going. Not only were his legs killing him from the tin shin guards he had foolishly fashioned and not only was he a nervous wreck from seeing that revolting monster spitting at him, but he had barely set eyes on Beth from the time he got out of the car. The day was by no means going the way he had planned. On top of that he had to piss so bad he could taste it, but he wasn't about to expose himself in this snake-infested territory.

The aching in his bladder began to replace the aching in his knees and the combination of discomforts folded him into a half-crouch-knees -together shuffle that had Clancy scratching his head.

"What are you doing, Sammy? You look like you're about to drop a foal."

"I can't help it. I've got to piss somethin' awful."

"Well, then, pull it out and piss. What's the big deal?" said Gordie.

"I can't. I can't go here 'cause she's liable to walk in. I ain't goin' to go wavin' it around in those woods with all them snakes around."

Gordie started laughing. "You got to be shitting me. There ain't a snake in this world with eyes good enough to see what you got. A bald eagle ain't got eyes that good. Now just get up the bank there and go."

Sammy's fear of wetting himself was rapidly overcoming his fear of snakes and he squiggled his way over to the edge of the woods and he began painfully climbing up the bank into the trees. He had no sooner disappeared into the growth than Donkey Nuts, Clevis and Beth arrived from the other side of the quarry platform.

"You guys have any luck?" Donkey Nuts asked.

"Yeah, Clancy nailed a four-footer, six buttons," Gordie said as he reached into the bag and pulled out the skin.

"I got a couple of prize winners myself," grinned Clevis as he reached into his burlap bag and pulled out a can of beer for each of them. "Where's Sam?"

"He went off to relieve himself. It ain't exactly been his day," Clancy said.

Sammy, meanwhile, had climbed about 20 feet up the bank to where he was hidden from view, carefully looked around and decided he was about as safe as he was going to get. He unzipped his pants and began to feel better than he had felt for hours as the pressure ran out of him. He had just finished when his foot began to slip and he stepped back. He felt something under his foot just as he saw something move on the ground between his legs. He let out a howl, turned so fast to run that he tangled his feet and fell backward. As he hit the ground he felt a sharp pain in the right cheek of his ass. He began screaming at the top of his lungs, thrashing about, flailing at the ground around him in a frantic attempt to get everything away from him. He was one tiny bundle of terror.

The others came running as soon as they heard the screams and they found Sammy thrashing around wildly, screaming, "I'm bit and I'm dead! I'm bit and I'm dead!"

"Wait, Sammy, wait. Calm down. What happened?" Gordie took his shoulder and tried to quiet him. "It got me! It got me! It's right there!" Sammy pointed wildly at the ground. They all looked but saw nothing.

"There ain't nothin' here, Sammy. What do you mean it got you? Where did it get you?"

"It got me on the ass. It took off. Oh God, I'm dead!" wailed Sammy.

"You better let us take a look," said Gordie. They were all alarmed now. "You don't mess with rattlesnake bites. Pull your pants down."

Sammy was aware of Beth standing there and hesitated for a second, but his fear overcame his modesty and he undid his belt and rolled over on his stomach. Gordie pulled his pants and shorts far enough down to see the two puncture wounds on his right cheek. "My God! He was right. He did get bit!" Gordie said. That sent Sammy into another spell of wailing.

"Well, we got to get that poison out quick. Donk, there ain't nothin' to do but suck it out."

"Donk? What are you tellin' me for?" said Donkey Nuts, looking distastefully at Sammy's unusually hairy ass. "I ain't no nurse."

"Clevis, how about you?" Gordie asked.

"Well, now, I wouldn't even know how you go about it. No sir, I don't suppose I would do the job right."

Clancy?

"I don't think it's the kind of thing I would be good at, either."

Gordie looked at Donkey Nuts again. "Donk, you're the one that was a Scout Master. You know all about cuttin' an X and all that. You've gotta do it."

"What about you? You got a bigger mouth than anybody. You do it."

"I never got past Tenderfoot. Don't you remember? You threw me out of the troop. I never even got to knot tying. You're the one that went to all the camporees."

"What do camporees have to do with suckin' poison out of a guy's ass?" Donkey Nuts wanted to know. "They do other things at camporees, silly stuff like playin' Simon Said and stuff like that. It didn't have nothin' to do with this."

Donkey Nuts knew perfectly well what to do. He had read about it enough times in the Scout manual and had taught it to kids in the troop. It was important information for kids living in this neck of the woods. But he just couldn't bring himself to put his mouth on that hairy old ass. Now, if it was Beth, it would be different, he thought to himself as he looked down on a half-naked Sammy moaning in the grass.

Gordie also knew perfectly well that Donkey Nuts knew what to do about a snake bite and he wouldn't let up. "You got to do it, Donk, and quick before he swells up like a dead bullfrog." Sammy let out a loud wail.

"Quiet, Sam, you don't want to upset yourself, makes the poison spread faster," Gordie said.

Sammy wailed again.

"You're goin' to kill him yourself with that talk," Donkey Nuts said disgustedly. He knew time was running against him and so were the arguments. Still, he had known Sammy a long time and he knew he probably hadn't had a bath in a week and God only knew where the ass had been over the past few years. Donkey Nuts had about as strong a stomach as anyone and was about as squeamish as a vulture, but the thought he was going to be sucking on Sammy's rear end was about all he could handle. He was working on another excuse when Beth said, "You have to do something. You can't just keep arguing about it. You're the leader, Maynard. You're the expert here. His life is in your hands."

Sammy wailed again.

It was the "Maynard" that did it. No one outside his family had called him that in years. And the way she said it made it even more personal than family. She was counting on him.

He took out his knife and knelt down by Sammy. He gathered the skin around the puncture wound between the thumb and finger of his left hand and made two quick slices through them. He knelt down and began sucking as the blood started to trickle from the cuts. He sucked for a second and then spat on the ground and then sucked again. He repeated this procedure several times, grimacing every time he had to return to Sammy's hide. He kept at it until he figured there couldn't be much blood, let alone poison, left in Sammy's system.

"That ought to do it," he said, getting to his feet. "We'll just let those cuts bleed out a little while we get him back to the house." He found himself turning his head and spitting repeatedly. He got a can of beer from Clevis and began gargling vigorously. "Is it OK for me to get up?" begged Sammy in a weak voice. "Somethin's sticking me in the belly."

Gordie started to lift him up. "It's no wonder, you're laying on a stick. Here, let me pull your pants up before someone sees somethin' they're not supposed to." He took hold of the back of Sammy's pants and yelped, "Ow!" He started shaking his hand in pain as a drop of blood popped out of the ends of two fingers. "What the hell you got in your pocket?"

"Those are the tins snips I was usin' to make my leggings. Did you cut yourself on them?"

Gordie looked at Donkey Nuts. Donkey Nuts looked at the punctures in the ends of Gordie's fingers. Then he looked at the tin snips that were now sticking out of Sammy's back pocket and then his face began to darken as the rage came welling up. Gordie, Clancy, Clevis and Beth quickly sneaked off down the bank before Donkey Nuts could see the shit-eating grins on their faces.

He was so furious that he barely heard a trembling Sammy say, "Thanks Donk, you saved my life."

GIVE ME THAT OLD TIME RELIGION

"BY GOD, SHE DIDN'T get me this time," Glenn Tink said as he hurried through the door, looking back over his shoulder. "She's goin' to have to find some other poor bastard to drag into Heaven today."

Glenn looked out the window of The Club and watched Abigail Detwiler look first at his pickup truck and then look up and down the street. After a couple of minutes and no sign of Tink, the portly matron hurried on down the street on her mission of mercy with the big sunshine basket on her arm that she had made up for Esther Rolland who was bedridden with the gout.

"She's got to be about the holiest woman I ever did come across and she's as tenacious as a damn snappin' turtle," Tink said. "She just don't let go."

What Abigail was trying to get a hold on to was Tink's immortal soul so she could steer him to the path of the righteous, but Tink wasn't buying. He was having too much fun.

Abigail Detwiler had made up her mind long since that anyone who would set foot in The Club was in dire need of saving and it was her calling to do what she could for the poor souls. She wasn't a preacher as such and, in fact, was a very nice 60-year-old graying woman who was probably the most active member of the First Baptist Church of Mill Town. She and her late husband had never been blessed with children so Abigail turned her energies toward the church and was always on the move doing good for someone in town.

Good for everyone except Catholics, that is. Abigail had no truck for the few Roman Catholics in town, regarding them as idol worshipers already beyond redemption. She was not about to waste her time on them. They had their own church and it was the wrong church and she didn't see much she could do about it. The non-believers in town, or more appropriately the non-churchgoers, were a different matter. They were fair game and Abigail declared open season on them. She wasn't pushy about it, but she never missed an opportunity to nudge one of them a little closer to the House of God, which in Abigail's case was a narrow white frame building in the center of town.

Most of The Club members, except for the likes of Ed Hooker, had at one time or another been the subject of an Abigail crusade. Some of these efforts didn't last for more than a couple of minutes or as long as it took her to realize she was wasting her time on a beery heathen. But some others, like Clancy Rierdon and Glenn Tink, had been Abigail targets for years, mostly because she had known members of their families to be straight backs who hearkened to the Word of the Lord. Abigail wasn't so much insistent as she was persistent. She didn't preach to anyone, she just suggested. But she did it every time she ran into the object of her conversion. She would meet redemption prospects in the bank, make a big fuss over their kids, complimenting them on anything remotely worth complimenting them on and getting them feeling real good. And then she would spoil it all by saying in front of everyone in the place, "Now, will we be seeing you at services Sunday morning?" It might be someone who hadn't seen the inside of a church in 40 years, but she would say it as though they hadn't missed a Sunday service since their baptism.

It may have been a comfortable question for those who did attend every Sunday, but for members of The Club who spent most Sunday mornings trying to remember what they did Saturday night, it was an awkward inquiry that prompted much hemming and hawing and usually ended with an "uh, well, uh, I'm not sure, but, uh, it depends, uh ..."

"Well, we'd love to see you," would be Abigail's parting words and the object of her quest would be left standing in front of everyone feeling like the biggest sinner in the world. It didn't matter that just about everyone else there had been subjected to the same humiliation. As a matter of fact, those who had been through it seemed to enjoy even more seeing someone else squirm.

Even the relatively devout townspeople felt a bit uneasy around Abigail and some of the holier ones felt dowright resentful. It was as though she was trying to corner the market on piety and freeze everyone else out. And they weren't to be frozen out, not by a damn sight. They could tuck a bible under their arms just as well as Abigail could and they could deliver their own casseroles to the needy. It was a real competition with a handful of them to see who could bring the most wayward sheep back to the flock. It was all done with smiles and kind words, but it was a bonafide battle among the Christian soldiers.

What stray lambs Abigail didn't manage to put the move on, the others did. It got so a good many people in town began wishing they were Catholics so they could be left alone. It went without saying that, if you weren't a Catholic, you were a Protestant and could be saved despite your sporadic, or lack of, attendance at church. Baptist, Methodist, Presbyterian, it didn't matter. As long as you weren't Catholic, you had some salvage value.

It was another biblical assault by Abigail that prompted Tink's remark at The Club about her having a lock on heaven. Glenn's mother had always been a good Baptist and Abigail couldn't see any reason why, with a good long chew on the Bible, Glenn couldn't make a reasonably good one also. So she kept after him, ignoring the fact that he had become weaned from formal religion in high school when he found out there was something a lot more fun to munch on.

Glenn was a decent young guy and after outgrowing a repulsive case of acne, became a moderately successful ladies man. He was not a major league stud, but was content to bang around in the minors, scoring on players who were mostly over the hill. As a matter of fact, most of them were more than over the hill, most of them had slid way down the other side. Glenn could get excited about almost anything in a skirt, but show him a grandma with gray in her hair and wrinkles in her skin and he was ready for action.

Glenn had no idea where his fixation for the geriatric set came from and gave little time to trying to figure it out. As best he could figure, it must have been Hazel Aiken, the wallpaper hanger. She had been doing the Tink family living room one day when Glenn was home from school on some pretense or other to avoid a chemistry exam he wasn't one bit ready for. He had kept pretty much to his room because that was where he had stashed the lingerie section of the Montgomery Ward catalog and several copies of Esquire magazine under his mattress. It also was where he kept his well-worn copy of God's Little Acre and his Marilyn Monroe calendar. His parents could not understand how he could spend all those hours in his room studying and still not seem to pass anything.

On this particular day Glenn's mother had gone to Binghamton shopping for the day and Glenn felt it safe to make several trips to the kitchen and the refrigerator. Early on he had noticed Hazel up on the step ladder with a long swath of wet paper hanging over her arm. Hazel had long since lost any semblance of curves to middle age and was sort of a lumpy soul, broad-shouldered and strong. She always worked in an old house dress that buttoned all the way up the front so that on hot days she could unbutton the neck as much as she needed to take in air. It also allowed her to unbutton the bottom as needed if she were going to be climbing up and down ladders all day. Some particularly hot and busy days she walked around with only a couple of the buttons in the middle holding the dress together. But with Hazel's looks no one bothered to give it a second thought or glance. No one that is except a horny teenage Glenn Tink who was desperate to know just what this thing was about women.

Hazel was not only coarse looking, she was coarse acting. She had been a rough cut from the start and had gotten tangled up at an early age with Darrell Aiken who was as rough cut as she was. About the best anyone in town could say about Darrell is that he was no prize but he could hang a straight roll of paper and could paint a ceiling without needing a drop cloth. He could do that if he could steer clear of the barrooms. It was not uncommon for Darrell to get paid for a job and then drop the whole wad over a bar before he ever made it home. Other than beating Darrell unmercifully a few times, Hazel put up with it until she and Darrell somehow produced a daughter. She figured it was time he cut out his shenanigans so she began accompanying him to work.

She'd bundle up the baby and put her in a food basket and tote her right along. If the baby started acting up, it didn't mean a thing to Hazel to unbutton that old housedress, haul out an over-sized breast and quiet the child down in front of whoever happened to be around. It didn't bother Darrell either. What bothered Darrell was having Hazel sitting there watching his every move. It made it a whole lot tougher for him to slide out to his beat-up old pickup truck and sample the bottle he had hidden behind the seat. Her watchful eye and his lack of alcohol got him into such a nervous state that he got so he couldn't do the trim around the windows without making a mess of everything. He finally resigned himself to the shakes and began painting both the trim and the window and then scraped the paint off the window with a razor blade. His papering eventually became as sloppy as his painting and his customers began to complain. The only times he regained his old artistry were the days that Hazel had to take the baby to the doctor and he was able to get to the stash behind the seat of the truck a dozen times a day. On those days he was Picasso, da Vinci and Michelangelo all rolled into one. His paint lines were straight and sure and you couldn't find the seams on his papering with reading glasses.

But those days became fewer and fewer as Hazel traipsed along with him from job to job and Darrell finally lost his inspiration all together. He got to shaking so bad that Hazel had to hold the step ladder when he was painting a ceiling.

One day she was holding the ladder when the baby began to wail. She turned to see what the problem was, let go of the ladder just as Darrell was about two-thirds of the way up with a bucket of paint in one hand and a brush in the other. The ladder began shaking and Darrell began flailing around on one leg. He began swinging his arms wildly in a sorry effort to regain his balance, forgetting that he had almost a full gallon of off-white on the end of one of them. The off-white splattered all over the Kelly green shag carpet and Darrell splattered all over an 1848 coffee table that had been preserved without a blemish for all those years. There wasn't much that could be salvaged of the coffee table and not much more that could be salvaged of Darrell. The doctor called it a herniated disc, but whatever it was was enough to lay Darrell up for good.

Hazel figured that whatever Darrell could do drunk she should be able to do sober so she just picked up where he left off. He sat home tending the baby while Hazel set out every morning with the truck, the ladders, the paper and paint. It wasn't long before she could do the job every bit as good as Darrell could and many in town thought she was much better. At least they knew she wasn't spending half her day rummaging around behind the seat of the truck. It did bother some of them that Hazel was such an earthy sort with a vocabulary seldom heard on the high seas. It was unnerving even for some of the men in town to hear Hazel say, "Where's your bathroom? I gotta take a shit." But she was such a good worker that they figured it was worth her steady stream of unladylike remarks.

It wasn't her language that Glenn was interested in that particular hooky-playing day when he walked through the living room with a snack and saw Hazel bending over stirring a bucket of paint. The top of her house dress was unbuttoned almost to her waist and Glenn was staring at cleavage he didn't even know existed. Hazel looked up. "What the hell's the matter with you? Ain't you never seen a tit before?" she asked.

Glenn just gulped. Hazel straightened up. "Here, make yourself useful and hold this ladder for me," she said. Glenn took a hold of the ladder as Hazel climbed to paint the ceiling. As she neared the top, she turned around to ask Glenn for a brush and he got his first close up of a woman's water works. Granted it was covered by a pair of oversized white panties but it was still Glenn's first crotch shot.

He was mesmerized. He forgot about the ladder, he forgot about his snack, he couldn't even have told you his name at that point. He just stood there staring into Hazel's crotch.

"Why, you horny little bastard. I bet you've never seen nothin' like that, have you? I bet you're cherry, aren't you?"

"Uh, no, not exactly," Glenn stammered, but then didn't know how to explain himself without embarrassing himself, so he shut up.

"You think you know what to do, do ya? Well, let's just see how much you know what to do," and Hazel stepped off the ladder and hauled him into his bedroom.

It was an experience that was to mark his preference in women for good. Despite his mediocre success with some of the less attractive girls in high school, Glenn's preference continued to run to older women and the more it ran, the older they got. Glenn's attraction to the geriatric was often discussed and analyzed at The Club, but no one ever made much sense out of it.

Donkey Nuts' reasoning on the situation was probably as close as anyone's. "He goes for them old bags 'cause they're just as desperate as he is. It gives him something in common with them."

Whatever the reason for his fixation it occupied most of his waking hours and some of his best dreams and it made him extremely uneasy around Abigail Detwiler. He always had the feeling that she knew what he was thinking. He knew she would never think about what he was always thinking about, but he still felt she knew and he dreaded it whenever she began her pitch.

So it was with great trepidation that he saw Abigail coming into the hardware store just as he was going out.

"Hello, Glenn, it's nice to see you. How are your mother and father?"

"They're fine, ma'am."

"I'm so glad to hear that. Your mother is a real saint,. She's the first one at service every Sunday and she sits right down in front. It's such a joy to see her there. I trust you'll be to the prayer meeting Monday night."

"Well, I don't know. I don't know but what I might have to take a load of hay to New Jersey Monday. But I'd sure like to be there if I could."

"This is one you won't want to miss, Glenn. The Wiggen family is going to be here singing gospel songs. They're nationwide famous and travel all over the country singing God's word. It should be a real inspiration and I certainly hope to see you there."

Glenn became hooked on hillbilly and gospel music while pounding hay truck up and down Route 11 and spent a good many hours pulled over to the side of the road swigging quarts of beer and listening to Wheeling, West Virginia and KDKA Pittsburgh.

He was talking in The Club about Abigail's godliness and her invitation to come hear some great gospel music when Danny Walsh walked in. Danny always enjoyed hearing about Glenn's brushes with Abigail, especially because of his own Catholic immunity.

Like most young Catholic men in the 1950s he wore a religious medal around his neck. Most the time he wore it under his shirt, but whenever he saw Abigail coming, he whipped it out and wore it on his chest like a clove of garlic. Abigail had known him since he was born and knew as well as anyone he was a Catholic, but he figured it didn't hurt to remind her.

He and Glenn were different in a whole lot of ways, but in two ways they were as close as identical twins – they loved good old country music and they would bang anything they could get their hands on without considering looks, size or age.

They had teamed up for any number of sexual disasters over the years but had never stopped trying. They were eternally optimistic that every woman in the world was after their bodies. Danny heard Glenn mention gospel music and immediately became interested.

"Who is this outfit and where can we go hear them?" he asked.

"They're a colored family called the Wiggens and they're going to be down to the Baptist church tonight," said Glenn.

"The Baptist church? Well, that leaves me out. Old Rev. Turner wouldn't let me anywhere near the place. He hates my guts. Besides, Catholics aren't allowed to go into a Protestant church. It's against the rules."

"Why is it against the rules?" Glenn wanted to know.

"Damned if I know. All I know is that it is a sin for me to go into a Protestant church. I don't think it is a big sin, but it's a sin all the same."

That got a lively religious discussion going in The Club about what is and isn't a sin and what should and shouldn't be a sin and the only thing that was concluded was that there couldn't be a whole lot more damage done to either Glenn or Danny by whatever church they walked in to.

After about a dozen cans of Stegmaiers apiece, Glenn and Danny agreed that some good rousing gospel music would make better Christian soldiers of both of them. They decided to at least go and stand outside the church and listen to as much music as they could hear.

They each tucked a fresh six-pack under their arms and headed down the street to the church. The sun had gone down while they were drinking up enough courage to undertake the venture and they tiptoed down the driveway in the dark alongside the church where they couldn't be seen but close enough to the open front door where they could hear reasonably well.

The Wiggens had gotten up a full head of steam and were "Amening" up a storm. The little church was fairly rocking with the driving rhythm of the music and the synchronized clapping of the congregation. A great sound was coming out of that front door and Glenn and Danny began a religious dance of their own in the shadows.

"Hot damn!" said Danny. "That music's almost worth becoming a Protestant!"

They swayed back and forth belching and farting to the best music they had heard in a while.

"You know what it must be like inside? It's got to be twice as good as out here," said Glenn. "Let's see if we can't just sneak in and stand in the back."

"Are you out of your mind? If old Rev. Turner sees me, he'll go nuts. He'll think his church is going to fall down."

"He won't even know we're in there. He's probably way down front anyway. We can just scrunch down in the back."

By this time the music and the beer had removed any fear Danny had about getting caught. The two of them went quietly up the steps and slid through the open door.

They were looking at the backs of the heads of about 200 people swaying back and forth clapping their hands in unison. Facing them down front were three overweight black women in white robes and a skinny black man in a red suit playing the biggest guitar they had ever seen. The women were singing at the tops of their lungs in perfect harmony with deep rich voices as pretty as any Glenn and Danny had ever heard.

The all-white congregation wasn't into shouting the Amens and Hallelujas all that well, but the Wiggens kept picking up the tempo and it wasn't long before an emotional frenzy had taken over the whole place. Some were crying, some were laughing and all of them were pulsating in a way seldom seen in the First Baptist Church of Mill Town.

Glenn and Danny were having a ball. They were bouncing up and down and clapping to the music and were enjoying themselves so much they forgot about the full cans of beer they had left hidden out by the front step. They were getting really cranked up and rolling. At the end of one song they waited expectantly for the Wiggens to start up on the next one. But the Wiggens walked to the back of the stage and sat down on some folding chairs. "What the hell they doing? They just got started," Danny whispered to Glenn.

"How should I know? I never been to one of these things," Glenn replied, himself annoyed that the music had stopped just as he was getting warmed up. The silence had also made them both aware that they were intruders on what was for all intents and purposes a private affair.

Rev. Turner didn't give the crowd much time to lose its emotional high. He began preaching with the same fire that the Wiggens had generated in their music and in no time at all was shouting at the top of his lungs that they were all headed for damnation unless they repented their sins and took God into their hearts.

"You must confess your sins to your brothers and sisters here tonight and cleanse your souls!" he shouted. "Confess and repent and be saved!"

"Old Rev.'s getting himself into a real lather, ain't he?" Glenn whispered to Danny as the bespectacled minister paced back and forth punching the air with both hands.

"He sure as hell is. I've never seen him act like that," said Danny, who was feeling more and more uncomfortable.

"My dear friends, come down here and be saved," Rev. Turner fairly begged the congregation. "Cast out your sins and be purified!" He began to sob and stretched his arms to the crowd. All of a sudden, mousey little Beatrice Tasker rose from her seat with tears streaming down her face and rushed to the front of the hall. "Praise God, I've sinned and I'm sorry," she cried. "I've sinned the sins of the flesh and I beg forgiveness." Beatrice's husband John was at first startled when his wife got up but now he was beginning to wonder what in the world she was talking about.

John couldn't even get her to take her clothes off in front of him let alone getting into any real good sins of the flesh. He was dumbfounded at first, but as Beatrice continued to fess up, he began wishing he could crawl under a rock.

"I have lusted for strange men," Beatrice wailed, her voice almost as thin as herself. "I have lusted for Emery Sliker and I have had wicked thoughts about Leonard Thomas. My body has been taken over with passion,. I am a sinner through and through."

"Old John must be shittin' his pants," said Danny after he and Glenn had recovered from the initial shock of hearing this plain, dull woman bare her soul.

"He ain't never going to be able to show his face in the barbershop again," agreed Glenn, who got to thinking about the passion she had claimed to have in that scrawny little body. Something to keep in mind, he told himself.

About the time Rev. Turner had assured Beatrice that she was now as holy as a saint, Gertrude Westcott was on her feet and heading down front. Danny and Glenn stared in astonishment at their former classmate. Gertrude Westcott was not much in the face, but she had a chest that went straight out in front of her and didn't come back. Every guy in school had agreed she had a pair as perfect as you could get and not one of them had been able to get within a foot of them. She was the coldest fish going, snooty and aloof. There were only two things desirable about her and no one had been able to get a hand on either one of them in school.

She now worked in old Charlie Ansell's law office and was as untouchable as ever, spending most of her evenings reading the Bible to her aunt Bernice.

Gertrude reached the front of the hall and turned to the congregation. "I need the Lord!" she cried. "My flesh has been weak!"

"Some weak," Danny said to Glenn. "She's got some of the strongest flesh going."

"I have fornicated with Warren Deemer and I am truly sorry," Gertrude wailed.

"Warren Deemer?" Glenn said out loud, "Warren Deemer? That seed?"

"I have rolled in the hay with a man like a common animal," Gertrude repented.

"That no-good barn boot bastard swore he never got next to her," Danny whispered angrily. "He said she was a regular ice cube."

"I never did trust Warren," replied Glenn, making a mental note to be sure to say hello to Gertrude the next time he saw her. Gertrude continued with a lot of other little sins that Glenn and Danny had no interest in and finally Rev. Turner cut her off by assuring her that God would understand about the roll in the hay and that she could start with a clean slate.

Most of the rest of the folks who began lining up to go forward and be saved were middle-aged sinners who had put in enough years to have at least managed to do enough things wrong to make the whole rigmarole worth while and Danny and Glenn began feeling real uncomfortable listening in on their confessions. But about the time they would make up their minds to sneak out the door, another young female wayward sheep would get up there and start laying out her tales of wickedness. That would draw their attention back to the front of the hall and they would listen stupefied to the revelations of sexual hanky panky that they had been missing out on. Mary Lou Gibbons, Barbara Cleary, Beverly Dibble all had at one time or another talked both Danny and Glenn out of their goals by telling them they had never done anything like that before and were saving themselves for their wedding days.

And now they were admitting they hadn't been saving themselves from hardly anyone except Glenn and Danny. On the one hand they were furious that they had been talked out of some good action, but on the other hand they were feeling good about having some new leads.

"That Mary Lou Gibbons doesn't know it, but I'm going to give her a chance to come right back here to the next meeting with a whole new story to tell," Glenn whispered to Danny.

"Yeah, well that Barbara has sent me home aching for the last time, too," Danny said. "I guess I'm as entitled as anybody is." The stream of repenters began to peter out and after one last futile effort to pry some of the more stubborn congregants out of their consciences, Rev. Turner turned the service back over to the Wiggens for a grand gospel finale.

Danny and Glenn had unconsciously inched their way forward during the confessing so they could better hear what the girls had been admitting to and when the music finally stopped they realized half the crowd was between them and the door. There was no way they were going to be able to sneak out.

They could do nothing but be herded along slowly up the aisle with the rest of God's sheep toward the front door where Rev. Turner had stationed himself to bid his flock goodnight. He shook hands with each of them as they filed out and urged them all to attend services the following Sunday. Glenn was in front of Danny and Rev. Turner pumped his hand and grasped his shoulder.

"It is so good to see you turn to the Lord, Glenn. I have just been waiting for the day God would steer you back to us. You can't know how it has pained me to see you chasing the Devil's tail. I knew a life of drinking and carousing was not for someone of the Tink stock. Praise God you've seen the right way."

The only way Glenn wanted to see was the way to the nearest decent sized tree where he could take a piss. All that beer he and Danny had downed earlier was now clamoring to get out. But Rev. Turner was not about to let Glenn go without reinforcing his message so he held his hand tight and continued to preach. The two of them blocked the doorway so no one else could get out of the church. By now everyone who had not make it out was bunched around Glenn staring at him while Rev. Turner made his pitch. Danny had also been blocked from getting out and was now standing within a foot of Rev. Turner, but the good reverend acted as though he was invisible. He looked right through Danny. This was almost as annoying to Danny as his swollen bladder was and he was beginning to lose his Irish temper.

Glenn kept trying to mutter a goodbye but was concentrating so hard on not wetting his pants and trying to ignore the stares that he could only manage a mumble.

"What is it, boy? What are you trying to say?" Rev. Turner glowed. "Don 't hold back, boy."

Glenn felt like a dam had burst in his lower gut and tried to talk between clenched teeth. All he could think of is that he had to go real bad.

"Don't be shy, son. These people are all rejoicing in your glory. Praise God you've come over. Let God give you the words to express the warmth that is spreading over you."

Glenn knew the only warmth that would be spreading over him would be all over the front of his pants if he didn't get out of there damn quick. He still couldn't do anything but moan as the pain worsened in his groin.

"Ah, yes, the spirit is in you, son. Say what you must say. Tell us what it is you want."

"What he wants is for you to get the hell out of his way before he pisses all over your leg," Danny snorted as he pushed Glenn past the speechless minister and the other stunned congregants.

Glenn was fumbling frantically for his fly as he fled down the steps with Danny right behind him. They had both hoped to make it to the big willow tree on the other side of the church driveway, but there was no way they were going to get that far. They managed to get to the middle of the driveway with their backs to the people before they whipped out their hoses and stood shoulder to shoulder sending two steady streams three feet in front of them. It was dark as they stood there and, although they were aware that everyone knew what they were doing, they were comforted with the knowledge that at least no one could see them.

That was until Rev. Turner's wife, not having any idea what was going on outside, flicked the switch on the garage flood light so that the congregants could make their way out to the sidewalk. All of a sudden Glenn and Danny were standing there in a light brighter than day with their tools pointing straight at Gertrude Westcott. It took her a couple of seconds to realize what she was looking at and then she let out a scream and headed out across the church lawn on a dead run for home.

The rest of the crowd stared for a moment at the spotlighted figures in the driveway and then began chattering: "Disgraceful! Sacrilege! In God's driveway!"

Glenn looked at Danny and Danny looked at Glenn. Danny shrugged his shoulders. "Screw 'em," he said as he slowly and deliberately zipped up his fly. Glenn did the same. Danny then walked over to the side of the curb and retrieved the cans of beer he and Glenn had stashed. He opened two cans, handed one to Glenn and said, "C'mon, let's go up to The Club and see if we can find us some nooky."

The crowd gasped again.

Danny and Glenn walked out of the brilliant light into the dark at the end of the driveway and turned up Main Street toward The Club.

"You know, I was really getting into that music," Danny said. Glenn smiled. He was thinking about Mary Lou Gibbons, Barbara Cleary and Beverly Dibble.

'TWAS A FOUL AND DIRTY DEED, INDEED

"I KNEW WHEN I saw him coming up the driveway that I should have gone right back in the barn and hid," Clevis Randall was saying to Johnny as Gordie Alley and Clancy Rierdon came into The Club on an unseasonably warm April afternoon. "But I didn't have the brains of a cow stuck in the muck so I stood right there and waited for him. Just plain dumb is what it was."

"Waited for who, Clevis?" Gordie asked. "What happened?"

"Ed Hooker, that thievin' old skunk. It's almost too embarrassing to talk about. I can't believe I got outwitted by a rock head who can't read, write or even tell time, but I did. And what really fries my ass is I practically saved his life that time he was getting the hell kicked out of him in."

"Hooker pulled a fast one on you?" Gordie couldn't believe it. Hooker had the brain and the ambition of a sloth and the others in The Club within hearing range of Clevis also became immediately interested.

Clevis may have been embarrassed to be telling on himself, but he also chuckled a bit as he began to explain.

"Well, I hadn't seen Ed in awhile, his bein' away in jail and all so I was kind of surprised to see him comin' up the road and I guess that's kind of what took me off guard. I thought he was still locked up."

About nine months earlier, and only a couple of weeks after Clevis had hauled him home in his trunk, Ed had managed to get a snootful in The Club late one night and decided he wanted to go to Big Bend. He staggered out of Johnny's and across the street to the darkness of the Cratter sawmill where a beat up old logging truck was parked. It was about a 1925 vintage rig that was used only for hauling things around the yard and had no license plates or head lights. The windshield was also gone and the fenders were so rusted away that they flapped in the wind. Old Dave Cratter never took the keys out of it because nobody in his right mind would get into the thing if he wasn't being paid to. But Dave didn't allow for old Ed.

At any rate, Ed climbed into the rust bucket and did his best to figure out how to make it work. Not being able to read or write, he had never been able to get a driver's license, but years of working as a farm hand had left him with a certain amount of experience around machinery. He had ruined more than one valuable piece of equipment before being booted off a half dozen farms, but not before he learned how to get an engine started. He hadn't learned much beyond that, but that was all he needed.

Ed turned on the key and that old truck started bucking across that lumber yard like a mustang. It would lurch a couple of feet and then gather itself and lurch again. Ed was getting a rather severe case of whiplash by the time it came to him that he had to push in the clutch. When he did that things smoothed out considerably and the engine burped, coughed, hiccupped and began running about as good as it was going to. It was a whole lot easier on Ed's neck, but he wasn't going anywhere, either. He just sat there with his foot to the floor and the engine screaming its lungs out, sparks flying out of the manifold. In the darkness it looked like someone had lit a campfire under the truck. The muffler had long since rusted into dust and the sound could be heard from one end of Main Street to the other.

Ed decided he was making more progress the other way so he took his foot off the clutch. That truck shot across the lumber yard like a Roman candle with the sparks shooting out the bottom, torching the sawdust as it went. Ed froze to the wheel and his foot jammed on the gas peddle as the old International made a bee line out of the sawmill and onto Main Street.

The truck had been left parked in second gear so it was able to crank up to about 35 miles an hour wide open as it howled through town on Route 11 toward Big Bend. It was long after midnight and well past the bedtime of most of the populace. It was as though the truck was tripping a series of switches as one house after another lit up in its wake as town folk tumbled out of bed to find out what the hell was going on.

The more resourceful half dozen or so called the state police barracks in the center of the borough and reported seeing some kind of flaming object flying past their houses. The descriptions varied widely and one hysterical caller swore that it was traveling about six feet off the ground.

Ed was unmindful of the commotion he was causing behind him. He was too fully occupied with what was in front of him. With no windshield to protect him he was fair game for every kind of night bug that could dart its way into his perpetually open mouth. They were coming at him fast and furious on this hot summer night and he was taking them in faster than he could spit them out. It didn't occur to him to close his mouth so he just kept gagging and spitting as one after another of them whacked his tonsils. All Ed knew is that he had a tiger by the tail, but it was headed in the right direction.

He had managed to get out of town and had covered about three of the five miles of Route 11 to Big Bend when the troopers in two cars caught up with him. They threw on their flashing lights and sirens, but it didn't mean a thing to Ed. There was no rear view mirror on the truck and the mufflerless engine easily drowned out the sirens.

Trooper Ron Core was in the lead pursuit car and Trooper Don McDonough was right behind him. Trooper Core was given to heroic actions so he cranked it up to 50 and pulled up alongside Ed. He threw Ed a fierce look and motioned him to pull over, but Ed ignored the command. It wasn't so much he ignored the command, he never saw it. He had his eyes and every bit of his attention riveted on the road just about three feet in front of the truck. He was too busy keeping that truck between the white lines to be noticing anyone else.

Trooper Core was not a peace officer to be ignored. He believed when he pinned that badge on his chest that he was due a large measure of respect and he made it clear to everyone in town that he was going to get it. He was so big that no one openly challenged him, but he was also so dumb that he was unaware of all the jokes going around town about him. Lots of people kidded about him, but no one questioned his courage or his willingness to take on a risky assignment.

He was ready to lay it all on the line when his second warning gesture to Ed went unheeded. After giving Ed plenty of time to respond, Trooper Core jerked the steering wheel to the right and rammed the brand new $2,500 Dodge cruiser right into the remains of the left front fender of the logging truck. Neither Ed nor the logging truck budged and Trooper Core found himself with the right front of his vehicle being crumpled into a mangled mess by the big front tire of the truck. Core was able to wrench the car away from the truck and immediately made another kamikaze pass at Ed, who hadn't yet realized there was anyone on the road except himself.

Between the alcohol and his concentration on keeping that truck headed straight toward Big Bend, he had all he could handle. Trooper Core slammed into the truck again, all but demolishing the police car and this time he hit with enough force to jar the truck off the side of the road. Ed held to his purpose and kept the truck going straight ahead. But this time straight ahead was straight across the front lawn of Justice of the Peace Art Beaver who lived right along Route 11 about two miles out of Big Bend. Art was real proud of the three rows of grapevines he had managed to keep alive along a 50-foot stretch of his yard and the cluster of prize-winning rose bushes just beyond them next to his driveway. In the summer everyone stopped to admire Art's roses.

The grape vines slowed Ed down a little as he uprooted them one right after the other and the rose bushes slowed him another notch as they came ripping out of the ground, but not enough to keep Ed from slamming broadside into Art's brand new gleaming white 1956 Cadillac.

The Cadillac was Art's pride and joy because it had been financed with all the inflated fines he had levied on out-of-town speeders. Troopers were known to travel across the county to bring their prisoners before Art. Art was a generous man and didn't mind sharing the wealth.

The Cadillac did bring Ed to a stop, but not before he had caved in the whole side of the thing and had shoved it into Art's tool shed, knocking it right off its foundation. Ed didn't even realize he was stopped until Trooper McDonough had whipped open the truck door, gun in hand and had ordered Ed out. Trooper Core, who had managed to get his demolished patrol car under control, also came running up to the truck, dropped into his shooting crouch, drew a bead on Ed and ordered him to freeze. Ed did the next best thing. He melted. He turned to see what all the commotion was about and slid off the truck seat, down the running board and onto the ground in a heap. His odyssey had come up about two and three quarters miles short of Big Bend.

Things didn't go too well for Ed in the judicial process that ensued, not so much because he stole the truck. That would only have constituted petty larceny. Art might even have been forgiving of the grapevines and the prize-winning roses. And he might even have seen some way to accept the mangled Cadillac. But it had been Ed's misfortune to whack that old Cadillac while Art was in the backseat in the prone position with the 20-year-old daughter of his next door neighbor. The crash had trapped the two of them and as frantically as Troopers Core and McDonough worked to free them, they were not able to do it before Art's wife had jumped out of bed, thrown on a robe and had rushed out to see what the ruckus was all about.

Art's embarrassment cost Ed six months in the county jail. Ed spent most of that six months going to the grocery store. The County Jail in Montross about six miles from Mill Town was not what could be called a maximum security prison. There was only the jailer and his wife, Norbert and Lena Durham, to watch over the 15 to 20 desperados who usually resided in the three-story brick building.

Lena saw to it that the inmates toed the mark while Norbert did the cooking and the laundry. Norbert was terrified of walking into the two cell blocks even when everyone was locked up as tight as Petey Slater's beer money. Norbert had heard what men locked up long enough would do to an innocent fellow who happened into their company.

Lena, on the other hand, had fantasies about what these hardcases might do to a woman if they got the chance and she spent a good part of the day in the cell blocks carelessly leaving cell doors open, particularly those housing the younger, better looking criminals. The truth be told, Lena had a lot less to worry about than Norbert. He was less than desirable to man or woman, but Lena was downright ugly. She was so ugly that, as soon as she walked into a cellblock, you could hear the cell doors slamming shut like a series or rifle shots. The inmates weren't locking themselves in, they were locking Lena out.

Ed had caused an immediate stir when he began his incarceration. He stunk. During the short period between his arrest and trial he had been kept in a holding cell in one corner of the jail and it hadn't occurred to anyone to make sure he took a shower. They hadn't even taken his grimy old clothes away from him. After his two-hour trial and sentencing, he was led into the main jail where he was issued dungarees and a blue prison shirt and was ordered into the latrine to shower and change clothes. Not daring to be alone with a naked inmate, Norbert just sent Ed in by himself and Ed simply went in, changed into his new blue outfit and rolled up his old clothes and tucked them under his arm and took them back to his cell to be kept secure until he was a free man again.

Ed hadn't been a full night on the cellblock before the complaints came rolling in. "Lena, somethin' died in here. Lena, you come drag it out."

"Whoooee, Did someone park the bone truck under the window? My Goddamn nostrils are cloggin' up."

"Norbert must be runnin' a paper mill in the bottom of this joint. It's enough to gag a maggot."

The complaints grew louder and louder until Lena finally had to order Ed out of the cellblock and back into the latrine. She stood right there while he climbed out of his prison outfit and stepped gingerly into the shower. He stood looking apprehensively up at the shower head as he took hold of one of the knobs. A spray of ice cold water hit him right in the face and he began howling at the top of his lungs, which only managed to half drown him as the water poured down his throat. It was beyond Ed's intellectual capacity to think to step out of the stream of water so he just stood there howling and choking. Lena couldn't take the noise any longer so she stepped over and turned on the hot water. But she did it just as Ed realized what was causing his agony and shut off the cold water.

From a shivering, shaking chunk of ice he suddenly became a dancing, steaming boiled lobster. He moved faster than he had ever moved in his life, but it was straight up and down. He kept hopping up and down with his hands cupped over his crotch hollering "Ooh! ooh! ooh!"

He was turning bright orange by the time Lena got the shower turned off completely. "I knew it," he whimpered. "I knew that stuff was no damn good for you."

What neither he nor Lena realized until later was that his record for avoiding soap was still intact.

Norbert Durham, in his infinite lack of ambition, had started what was probably the first prison release program in Pennsylvania. It was basically a self release program. Shortly after taking on the weighty responsibility of jailer, Norbert had found that the demands were almost beyond him. Prisoners wanted cigarettes, they wanted candy, they wanted magazines and they wanted to be fed three times a day. No one had warned him of all this and he felt put upon, indeed. After running to the store several times for cigarettes and groceries, he decided enough was enough. They were the prisoners. Why was it they got to sit around all the time while he did the work? "From now on," he said, "If you want something, you can get it yourself."

He quickly instituted a system whereby a prisoner who wanted something that wasn't in supply would be sent to the store to get it himself. If it was groceries, the money would come out of the jail budget, but each prisoner was expected to buy his own cigarettes. He wasn't allowed to bring any beer except on Saturdays and then he was expected to share. The more resourceful prisoners quickly learned how to shave a nickel here and a nickel there from the grocery money and sneak into the kitchen of the Naughton Hotel for a couple of beers before returning to the jail.

Ed wasn't one of the more resourceful prisoners and he couldn't count or read worth a damn and Norbert quickly learned that he could send Ed downtown with a grocery list and money and he would come back with exactly what he was sent for. All he did was hand the list and the change purse to the store clerk and wait for him to fill the order.

He hadn't been an inmate long before Norbert had him doing most of the shopping. The other inmates didn't mind because the longer he was out of the cellblock, the easier it was to breathe. Ed settled into a steady errand-running routine and Norbert was kind of sorry to see him go at the end of his half-year term because now it meant he had to do the shopping himself or try to outwit the inmates who kept shaving the grocery money on him.

At any rate, Ed's release date did arrive and he climbed back into his still unwashed old clothes, walked to the outskirts of Montross and caught a ride on the back of a cattle truck back to Mill Town. He had paid his debt to society and was a free man. "I knew Ed was out," Clancy was saying as Clevis poured himself another beer. "I saw him down behind the American store rootin' through the garbage. He had more flies around him than the garbage can did."

"Well, I wish I'd known it," said Clevis. "Like I say, he kind of took me by surprise so I just stood there and waited for him." By now everyone in The Club was listening as Clevis related what happened next.

It had been one of those brief warm spells in April when everyone got the false hope that the chill had gone for good and that it was nothing but warm days ahead. Clevis had been able to get to the outside work for only a couple of days and was tackling it with enthusiasm. It was always a good feeling to start gearing up for the summer and Clevis went at it as hard as anybody.

He had been needing a break when Ed came walking down the road and up his driveway, and being about as friendly a man as there was in the county, Clevis wasn't above stopping to say hello to Ed.

"Well, Ed, you don't look any the worse for six months of concrete and steel."

"Hell, Clevis, you know me, ain't any jail in this state gonna give me no trouble. Ain't a jail in this state can hold me, either. Only reason I stayed is 'cause it was a good place to winter."

"I dunno, I bet there were some mighty hard cases in there. Bet you must have been at least a little bit nervous."

"Me? hell no, Didn't none of them mess with me. Someone must have spread the word about me before I got there. There wasn't a one of them that even dared get near me."

"Well, It's good to see you out, anyway, Ed. What brings you down my road?"

Nothin' really. I was walkin' down to the Arlington Hotel and decided to take the old road instead of that damn three-lane. A guy could get killed on that."

The road that Clevis lived on ran parallel to Route 11 and had once been the only road between Mill Town and Big Bend, but now the only people who used it were the ones who lived on it. Clevis suspected Ed was using the old road for two reasons. One was that no one in his right mind would give him a ride so there was no advantage in taking the heavily traveled three-lane and secondly he did not want to get any closer to Art Beaver's house than he had to.

"You got yourself a pretty good hike," Clevis said. You're going to be about dried up by the time you get to the Arlington. You'll drink that place dry."

"And don't you think I can 't do it, too," said Ed. "But I sure could use a little snort of something right now. You put up any hard cider in the fall?"

"Does a cow piss in the creek? When did you ever know me not to put up hard cider? I got a couple of barrels in the store room that would have your dobber twitchin' in a second."

"Yeah? Have you tried it yet?"

"No, but I added about 25 pounds of honey to each one of 'em and if that wouldn't set your ears to ringin', I don't know what would."

"Well, what do you say we give it a try. I'm dryer than old Harry." "I'll tell you, Ed, I would be happy to, but I was just gettin' a good start on puttin' in a new septic tank and my woman ain't goin' to give me a moment's peace, or a piece of anything else, until I got it done."

"Hell, Clevis, I'll help you with it. Let's just test a glass or two of that stuff and then I'll get right in there and we'll have that tank in the ground in no time."

Clevis knew very well that the only thing Ed Hooker detested more than soap and water was hard work. But he was kind of interested in seeing how his new batch had come out and figured it wouldn't hurt to draw off a pint or two. He went into the storeroom and got a couple of pint jars, rinsed them out and drew off about a half a pint apiece of the clearest, tangiest cider he had made in a long time. He sat down under the big willow in the front yard and invited Ed to join him. They each took a long swig and smacked their lips.

"Hot damn, Clevis, that is just about the finest cider I ever drank. Those Frenchies couldn't make anything taste better than this."

"It is a particular good batch," said Clevis, "I can feel my ears warmin' already. That honey must of kicked the alcohol up pretty good." They sat and chugged and chatted until their jars were empty. "You only about half filled that jar, Clevis. Suppose we could have just a little bit more?"

Clevis knew he was making a mistake, but he had such a good feeling warming his insides, he went ahead and said yes. "You fetch it this time, Ed. Just make sure you turn the spigot off tight."

Ed got up and walked over to the storeroom where he proceeded to fill each of the jars to the top. He returned and sat down by Clevis. "My God, Ed, I ain't never goin' to be able to finish all this, and you can't drink half as much as I can." "What are you talkin' about? I pour this much on my oatmeal," bragged Ed. Clevis knew better. Two beers and Ed was bouncing off the walls. "Hell, Clevis I've seen you drink this much in one swallow."

"Not of this stuff, you haven't. This stuff has got to be 60-70 proof.

"Well, it sure don't taste 70 proof. It's smooth as the top of Sammy Griney's head. Goes down like water."

He was right there. It was easy drinking and much to Clevis's surprise it wasn't long before he had finished his jar and Ed was also sitting there with an empty one. Clevis was seeing clear, thinking clear but when he agreed to get refills he found that he not only couldn't stand up, he couldn't even move his legs.

"Damn, this stuff has a kick," he said. "I feel fine, but I'm paralyzed.

"Paralyzed,? You ain't paralyzed, you just don't want to have to fetch the next round," said Ed, watching Clevis closely.

"I'm not lyin, I can't get a leg under me," said Clevis.

"You sure about that?"

"Yeah, I'm sure. How you feelin'?"

"Well, I feel just fine, I'll get a couple more," said Ed as he stood up and walked steady as a rock to the storeroom.

He came back with two more jars full and handed one to Clevis. He set his down and headed down Clevis's driveway.

"Where the hell you goin'?" and it began to dawn on Clevis that Ed Hooker had no business being conscious let alone walking steady after all that cider.

Ed got to the road and waved his arm and a minute later a pickup truck came round the corner. Ed climbed on the running board as the truck began to back up Clevis's driveway. It backed right straight up to the storeroom. As it passed Clevis he could see Ed's brother, Herbie, grinning out the window at him. Clevis was able to function just about enough to turn around and see them loading one of his barrels into the back of the truck. "You bastard, Ed. You come back with my cider right now," Clevis shouted as he tried in vain to raise himself up on one arm. All he managed to do was get the sleeve of his shirt soaking wet in the puddle of cider that saturated the ground next to where Ed had been sitting, and to shake a quickly numbing fist at the truck disappearing down the old road to Big Bend.